Noises Off

A PLAY IN THREE ACTS

by

Michael Frayn

SAMUEL FRENCH

FOUNDED 1830

New York Hollywood London Toronto

SAMUELFRENCH.COM

ISBN 978-0-573-61969-4   Printed in U.S.A.   **#16052**

IMPORTANT BILLING AND CREDIT REQUIREMENTS

All producers of *NOISES OFF must* give credit to the Author of the Play in all programs distributed in connection with performances of the Play, and in all instances in which the title of the Play appears for the purposes of advertising, publicizing or otherwise exploiting the Play and /or a production. The name of the Author *must* appear on a separate line on which no other name appears, immediately following the title and *must* appear in size of type not less than fifty percent of the size of the title type.

Billing must be substantially as follows:

(NAME OF PRODUCER)
presents

NOISES OFF

by

MICHAEL FRAYN

Noises Off
BY
Michael Frayn

was first presented, by arrangement with Michael Codron,
at the Lyric Theatre, Hammersmith,
on 23 February 1982,
and on 31 March 1982 by Michael Codron
at the Savoy Theatre, London.

The Cast:

Dotty Otley	Patricia Routledge
Lloyd Dallas	Paul Eddington
Garry Lejeune	Nicky Henson
Brooke Ashton	Rowena Roberts
Poppy Norton-Taylor	Yvonne Antrobus
Frederick Fellowes	Tony Mathews
Belinda Blair	Jan Waters
Tim Allgood	Roger Lloyd Pack
Selsdon Mowbray	Michael Aldridge
Electrician	Ray Edwards

Directed by Michael Blakemore
Designed by Michael Annals
Lighting by Spike Gaden

Noises Off
BY
Michael Frayn

opened on Broadway at the Brooks Atkinson Theatre,
presented by James M. Nederlander, Robert Fryer,
Jerome Minskoff, The Kennedy Center, and
Michael Codron in association with
Jonathan Farkas and MTM Enterprises, Inc.,
on December 11, 1983.

The Cast:

Dotty Otley	Dorothy Loudon
Lloyd Dallas	Brian Murray
Garry Lejeune	Victor Garber
Brooke Ashton	Deborah Rush
Poppy Norton-Taylor	Amy Wright
Frederick Fellowes	Paxton Whitehead
Belinda Blair	Linda Thorson
Tim Allgood	Jim Piddock
Selsdon Mowbray	Douglas Seale

Directed by Michael Blakemore
Settings and Costumes Designed by Michael Annals
Lighting Designed by Martin Aronstein
Casting by Howard Feuer and Jeremy Ritzer
Production Stage Manager - Susie Cordon
Stage Manager – Laura deBuys

Noises Off

BY

Michael Frayn

was revived in its present form by the Royal National Theatre,
in association with
Ambassador Theatre Group and Act Productions Ltd.
It previewed in the Lyttleton Theatre on 29 September 2000
and opened on 5 October 2000.

The Cast:

Dotty Otley	Patricia Hodge
Lloyd Dallas	Peter Egan
Garry Lejeune	Aden Gillett
Brooke Ashton	Natalie Walter
Poppy Norton-Taylor	Selina Griffiths
Frederick Fellowes	Jeff Rawle
Belinda Blair	Susie Blake
Tim Allgood	Paul Thornley
Selsdon Mowbray	Christopher Benjamin

Directed by Jeremy Sams

Designed by Robert Jones
Lighting by Tim Mitchell
Sound by Fergus O'Hare *for Aura*

☙ ☙ ☙ ☙

On 14 May 2001 this production opened at the
Piccadilly Theatre, London, with the same cast except for:

Dotty Otley	Lynn Redgrave
Garry Lejeune	Stephen Mangan

THE ROYAL NATIONAL THEATRE PRODUCTION OF

Noises Off

BY

Michael Frayn

opened again on Broadway at the Brooks Atkinson Theatre,
presented by
Ambassador Theatre Group and Act Productions,
Waxman Williams Entertainment, D. Harris/M. Swinsky,
USA Ostar Theatricals and Nederlander Presentations,
on November 1, 2001.

The Cast:

Dotty Otley	Patti Lupone
Lloyd Dallas	Peter Gallagher
Garry Lejeune	Thomas McCarthy
Brooke Ashton	Katie Finneran
Poppy Norton-Taylor	Robin Weigert
Frederick Fellowes	Faith Prince
Belinda Blair	Edward Hibbert
Tim Allgood	T.R. Knight
Selsdon Mowbray	Richard Easton

Directed by Jeremy Sams

Sets and Costumes by Robert Jones

Lighting by Tim Mitchell   *Sound by* Fergus O'Hare *for Aura*

Casting by Jim Carnahan   *Technical Supervision* by Unitech

Production Stage Manager - David O'Brien

Press Representative - Barlow-Hartman   *Marketing* - TMG

General Management - 101 Productions, Ltd.

Associate Producers
Pre-Eminence   Incidental Colman Tod   Curtis/Johnson

AUTHOR'S NOTE

This play has gone through many different forms and versions. Here, to avoid any mysteries or confusions, is a brief history.

It began life as a short one-acter entitled *Exits*, commissioned by the late Martin Tickner, for a midnight matinee of the Combined Theatrical Charities at the Theatre Royal, Drury Lane, on 10 September 1977, where it was directed by the late Eric Thompson, and played by Denis Quilley, Patricia Routledge, Edward Fox, Dinsdale Landen and Polly Adams. Michael Codron thereupon commissioned a full-length version, and waited for it with intermittent patience. Michael Blakemore, the director, persuaded me to rethink and restructure the resulting text, and suggested a great many ideas which I incorporated.

After the play had opened at the Lyric, Hammersmith, in 1982, I did a great deal more rewriting. I went on rewriting, in fact, until Nicky Henson, who was playing Garry, announced on behalf of the cast (rather as Garry himself might have done) that they would learn no further versions.

The play transferred to the Savoy Theatre and ran until 1987, with five successive casts. For two of the cast changes I did more rewrites. I also rewrote for the production in Washington in 1983, and I rewrote again when this moved to Broadway.

Reading the English text that has been in use in the past decade and a half I have discovered a series of bizarre misprints, and I suspect that directors have been driven to some quite outlandish devices to make sense of them. What's happened to it in other languages I can for the most part only guess. I know that in France it has been played under two different titles (sometimes simultaneously), and in Germany under four. I imagine that it's often been freely adapted to local circumstances, in spite of the prohibitions in the contract. In France, certainly, my British actors and the characters they are playing turned into Frenchmen, in Italy into Italians (who introduced a 'Sardine Song' between the acts). In Barcelona they were Catalan-speaking actors playing Spanish-speaking characters; in Tampere, in northern Finland, they were robust northerners speaking the Tampere dialect and playing effete southerners with Helsinki accents. On the Japanese poster they all appear to be Japanese; on the Chinese poster Chinese. In Prague they performed the play for some ten years without Act Three, and no one noticed until I arrived.

For the revival at the National Theatre in 2000 I've rewritten yet again. Some of the changes are ones that I've been longing to make myself—there's nothing like having to sit through a play twelve million times to make your fingers itch for the delete key. Many other changes were suggested by the radical criticisms and irresistible inventions of my new director, Jeremy Sams. I hope that no one will consciously notice the difference, but if I have demolished any particularly cherished errors or suggestive inconsistencies I apologize.

SETTING

Act I

The living room of the Brents' country home.
Wednesday afternoon.

(Grand Theatre, Weston-super-Mare.
Monday, January 14th.)

Act II

The living room of the Brents' country home.
Wednesday afternoon.

(Theatre Royal, Ashton-under-Lyne.
Wednesday matinee, February 13.)

Act III

The living room of the Brents' country home.
Wednesday afternoon.

(Municipal Theatre, Stockton-on-Tees.
Saturday, April 6.)

The cast of *Noises Off* is performing a play called **Nothing On.**
Sample pages for the program for **Nothing On** at The Grand Theatre,
Weston-super-Mare, are provided on pages 173 – 181.

ACT I

The living room of the Brents' country home. Wednesday afternoon.
(Grand Theatre, Weston-super-Mare, Monday January 14.)
From the estate agent's description of the property: A delightful 16th-century posset mill, 25 miles from London. Lovingly converted, old-world atmosphere, many period features. Fully equipped with every aid to modern living, and beautifully furnished throughout by owner now resident abroad. Ideal for overseas company seeking perfect English setting to house senior executive. Minimum three months let. Apply sole agents: Squire, Squire, Hackham and Dudley.

The accommodation comprises: an open-plan living area, with a staircase leading to a gallery. A notable feature is the extensive range of entrances and exits provided. On the ground floor the front door gives access to the mature garden and delightful village beyond. Another door leads to the elegant paneled study, and a third to the light and airy modern service quarters. A fourth door opens into a luxurious bathroom/WC suite, and a full-length south-facing window affords extensive views. On the gallery level is the door to the master bedroom, and another to a small but well-proportioned linen cupboard. A corridor gives access to all the other rooms in the upper parts of the house. Another beautifully equipped bathroom/WC suite opens off the landing halfway up the stairs.

All in all, a superb example of the traditional English set-builder's craft — a place where the discerning theatregoer will feel instantly at home.

(Introductory music. As the curtain rises, the award-winning modern

telephone is ringing.
Enter from the service quarters MRS. CLACKETT, a housekeeper of
character. She is carrying an imposing plate of sardines.)

MRS. CLACKETT. It's no good you going on. I can't open sardines *and* answer the phone. I've only got one pair of feet. *(She puts the sardines down on the telephone table by the sofa, and picks up the phone.)* Hello... Yes, but there's no one here, love... No, Mr. Brent's not here... He lives here, yes, but he don't live here now because he lives in Spain... Mr. Philip Brent, that's right... The one who writes the plays, that's him, only now he writes them in Spain... No, she's in Spain, too, they're all in Spain, there's no one here... Am *I* in Spain? No, I'm not in Spain, dear. I look after the house for them, but I go home at one o'clock on Wednesday, only I've got a nice plate of sardines to put my feet up with, because it's the royal what's it called on the telly — the royal you know — where's the paper, then...? *(She picks up the newspaper lying on the sofa and searches in it.)* ... And if it's to do with letting the house then you'll have to ring the house-agents, because they're the agents for the house... Squire, Squire, Hackham and who's the other one...? No, they're not in Spain, they're next to the phone in the study. Squire, Squire, Hackham, and hold on, I'll go and look. *(She replaces the receiver. Or so the stage directions say in Robin Housemonger's play,* 'Nothing On'. *In fact, though, she puts the receiver down beside the phone instead.)* Always the same, isn't it. Soon as you take the weight off your feet, down it all comes on your head. *(Exit MRS. CLACKETT into the study, still holding the newspaper. Or so the stage-direction says. In fact she moves off holding the plate of sardines instead of the newspaper.)*

(As she does so, DOTTY OTLEY, the actress who is playing the part of MRS. CLACKETT, comes out of character to comment on the move.)

DOTTY. And I take the sardines. No, I leave the sardines. No, I take the sardines.

(The disembodied voice of LLOYD DALLAS, the director of 'Nothing

On', *replies from somewhere out in the darkness of the auditorium.)*

LLOYD. You leave the sardines, and you put the receiver back.
DOTTY. Oh yes, I put the receiver back.

(She puts the receiver back, and moves off again with the sardines.)

LLOYD. And you leave the sardines.
DOTTY. And I *leave* the sardines?
LLOYD. You *leave* the sardines.
DOTTY. I put the receiver back and I leave the sardines.
LLOYD. Right.
DOTTY. We've changed that, have we, love?
LLOYD. No, love.
DOTTY. That's what I've always been doing?
LLOYD. I shouldn't say that, Dotty, my precious.
DOTTY. How about the words, love? Am I getting some of them right?
LLOYD. Some of them have a very familiar ring.
DOTTY. Only it's like a fruit machine in there.
LLOYD. I know that, Dotty.
DOTTY. I open my mouth, and I never know if it's going to come out three oranges or two lemons and a banana.
LLOYD. Anyway, it's not midnight yet. We don't open till to-morrow. So you're holding the receiver.
DOTTY. I'm holding the receiver.
LLOYD. 'Squire, Squire, Hackham, and hold on...'

(DOTTY resumes her performance as MRS. CLACKETT.)

MRS. CLACKETT. Squire, Squire, Hackham, and hold on, don't go away, I'm putting it down. *(She replaces the receiver.)* Always the same, isn't it. Put your feet up for two minutes, and immediately they come running after you.

(Exit MRS. CLACKETT into the study, still holding the newspaper. Only she isn't holding the newspaper.

The sound of a key in the lock.)

    LLOYD. Hold it.

(The front door opens. On the doorstep stands ROGER, holding a cardboard box. He is about thirty, and has the well-appointed air of a man who handles high-class real estate.)

    ROGER. ... I have a housekeeper, yes, but this is her afternoon off.
    LLOYD. Hold it, Garry. Dotty!

(Enter VICKI through the front door. She is a desirable property in her early twenties, well-built and beautifully maintained throughout.)

    ROGER. So we've got the place entirely to ourselves.
    LLOYD. Hold it, Brooke. Dotty!

(Enter DOTTY from the study.)

    DOTTY. Come back?
    LLOYD. Yes, and go out again with the *newspaper.*
    DOTTY. The newspaper? Oh, the newspaper.
    LLOYD. You put the receiver back, you leave the sardines, and you go out with the newspaper.
    GARRY. Here you are, love.
    DOTTY. Sorry, love.
    GARRY. *(Embraces her.)* Don't worry, love. It's only the technical.
    LLOYD. It's the dress, Garry, honey. It's the dress rehearsal.
    GARRY. So when was the technical?
    LLOYD. So when's the dress? We open tomorrow!
    GARRY. Well, we're all thinking of it as the technical. *(To DOTTY.)* Aren't we, love?
    DOTTY. It's all those words, my sweetheart.
    GARRY. Don't worry about the words, Dotty, my pet.

DOTTY. Coming up like oranges and lemons.

GARRY. Listen, Dotty, your words are fine, your words are better than the, do you know what I mean? *(To BROOKE.)* Isn't that right?

BROOKE. *(Her thoughts elsewhere.)* Sorry?

GARRY. *(To DOTTY.)* I mean, OK, so he's the, you know. Fine. But, Dotty, love, you've been playing this kind of part for, well, you know what I mean.

LLOYD. All right? So Garry and Brooke are off, Dotty's holding the receiver...

GARRY. No, but here we are, we're all thinking, my God, we open tomorrow, we've only had a fortnight to rehearse, we don't know where we are, but my God, here we are!

DOTTY. That's right, my sweet. Isn't that right, Lloyd?

LLOYD. Beautifully put, Garry.

GARRY. No, but we've got to play Weston-super-Mare all the rest of this week, then Yeovil, then God knows where, then God knows where else, and so on for God knows how long, and we're all of us feeling pretty much, you know... *(To BROOKE.)* I mean, aren't *you?*

BROOKE. Sorry?

LLOYD. Anyway, you're off, Dotty's holding the receiver...

GARRY. Sorry, Lloyd. But sometimes you just have to come right out with it. You know?

LLOYD. I know.

GARRY. Thanks, Lloyd.

LLOYD. OK, Garry. So you're off...

GARRY. Lloyd, let me just say one thing. Since we've stopped. I've worked with a lot of directors, Lloyd. Some of them were geniuses. Some of them were bastards. But I've never met one who was so totally and absolutely... I don't know...

LLOYD. Thank you, Garry. I'm very touched. Now will you get off the fucking stage? *(Exit GARRY through the front door.)* And, Brooke...

BROOKE. Yes?

LLOYD. Are you in?

BROOKE. In?

LLOYD. Are you there?

BROOKE. What?

LLOYD. You're out. OK. I'll call again. And on we go. *(Exit BROOKE through the front door.)* So there you are, holding the receiver.

DOTTY. So there I am, holding the receiver. I put the receiver back and I leave the sardines.

MRS. CLACKETT. Always the same story, isn't it...

LLOYD. And you take the newspaper.

(She comes back, and picks up the newspaper and the receiver.)

DOTTY. I leave the sardines, I take the newspaper.

MRS. CLACKETT. Always the same story, isn't it. It's a weight off your mind, it's a load off your stomach.

DOTTY. And off at last I go.

LLOYD. Leaving the receiver.

(She replaces the receiver and goes off into the study. Enter ROGER as before, with the cardboard box.)

ROGER. ... I have a housekeeper, yes, but this is her afternoon off. *(Enter VICKI as before.)* So we've got the place entirely to ourselves. *(ROGER goes back and brings in a flight bag, and closes the front door.)* I'll just check. *(He opens the door to the service quarters. VICKI gazes round.)* Hello? Anyone at home? *(Closes the door.)* No, there's no one here. So what do you think?

VICKI. Great. And this is all yours?

ROGER. Just a little shack in the woods, really. Converted posset mill. Sixteenth-century.

VICKI. It must have cost a bomb.

ROGER. Well, one has to have somewhere to entertain one's business associates. Someone coming at four o'clock, in fact. Arab sheikh. Oil. You know.

VICKI. Right. And I've got to get those files to our Basingstoke office by four.

ROGER. Yes, we'll only just manage to fit it in. I mean, we'll only just do it. I mean...

VICKI. Right, then.

ROGER. *(Putting down the box and opening the flight bag.)* We won't bother to chill the champagne.

VICKI. All these doors!

ROGER. Oh, only a handful, really. *(He opens the various doors one after another to demonstrate.)* Study... Kitchen.. And a self-contained service flat for the housekeeper.

VICKI. Terrific. And which one's the ... ?

ROGER. What?

VICKI. You know ...

ROGER. The usual offices? Through here.

(He opens the downstairs bathroom door for her.)

VICKI. Fantastic.

(Exit VICKI into the bathroom. Enter MRS. CLACKETT from the study, without the newspaper.)

MRS. CLACKETT. Now I've lost the sardines ...

(Mutual surprise. ROGER closes the door to the bathroom, and slips the champagne back into the bag.)

ROGER. I'm sorry. I thought there was no one here.

MRS. CLACKETT. I'm not here. I'm off, only it's the royal you know, where they wear those hats, and they're all covered in fruit, and who are you?

ROGER. I'm from the agents.

MRS. CLACKETT. From the agents?

ROGER. Squire, Squire, Hackham and Dudley.

MRS. CLACKETT. Oh. Which one are you, then? Squire, Squire, Hackham, or Dudley?

ROGER. I'm Tramplemain.

MRS. CLACKETT. Walking in here as if you owned the place! I thought you was a burglar.

ROGER. No, I just dropped in to ... go into a few things... *(The bathroom door opens. ROGER closes it.)* Well, to check some of the measurements... *(The bathroom door opens. ROGER closes it.)* Do one or two odd jobs... *(The bathroom door opens. ROGER closes it.)* Oh, and a client, I'm showing a prospective tenant over the house.

(The bathroom door opens.)

VICKI. What's wrong with this door?

(ROGER closes it.)

ROGER. She's thinking of renting it. Her interest is definitely aroused.

(Enter VICKI from bathroom.)

VICKI. That's not the bedroom.
ROGER. The bedroom? No, that's the downstairs bathroom and WC suite. And this is the housekeeper, Mrs. Crockett.
MRS. CLACKETT. Clackett, dear, Clackett.
VICKI. Oh. Hi.
ROGER. She's not really here.
MRS. CLACKETT. Only it's the royal, you know, with the hats.
ROGER. *(To MRS. CLACKETT.)* Don't worry about us.
MRS. CLACKETT. *(Picks up the sardines.)* I'll have the sound on low.
ROGER. We'll just inspect the house.
MRS. CLACKETT. Only now I've lost the newspaper.

(Exit MRS. CLACKETT into the study, carrying the sardines. Only she leaves them behind.)

LLOYD. Sardines!
ROGER. I'm sorry about this.
VICKI. That's all right. We don't want the television, do we?
LLOYD. Sardines!

(Enter DOTTY from the study.)

DOTTY. I've forgotten the sardines.

GARRY. Lloyd! These sardines! They're driving us all mad!

LLOYD. Something wrong with the sardines? Poppy!

GARRY. There's four plates of sardines coming on in Act One alone! They go here, they go there. *She* takes them — *I* take them. *(To BROOKE.)* I mean, don't *you* feel, you know?

BROOKE. *(Elsewhere again.)* Sorry?

GARRY. The sardines.

BROOKE. What sardines?

(Enter POPPY, the assistant stage manager, from the wings.)

POPPY. Change the sardines?

LLOYD. Make it four grilled turbot. Off the bone.

GARRY. *(To LLOYD.)* OK, it's all right for you. You're sitting out there. We're up here. We've got to *do* it. Plus we've got bags, we've got boxes. Plus doors. Plus words. You know what I mean?

DOTTY. We're not getting at you, Poppy, love. We think the sardines are lovely.

GARRY. I'm just trying to, you know.

LLOYD. So what *do* you want to change, Garry? The bags? The boxes? The doors?

DOTTY. We can't start *changing* things now, love!

GARRY. I'm just *saying*. Words. Doors. Bags. Boxes. Sardines. *Us*. OK? I've made my point?

LLOYD. You certainly have, Garry. Got that, Poppy?

POPPY. Um. Well.

LLOYD. Right. On we go. From Dotty's exit. And Poppy...

POPPY. Yes?

LLOYD. Don't let this happen again.

POPPY. Oh. No.

(Exit POPPY into the wings.)

GARRY. Sorry, Lloyd. I just thought we ought to, do you know what I mean?

    LLOYD. Of course.

    GARRY. Better out than, you know.

    LLOYD. Much better. As long as Dotty's happy.

    DOTTY. Absolutely happy, Lloyd, my love.

(She goes to the study door.)

    LLOYD. Will you do something for me then, Dotty, my precious?

    DOTTY. Anything, Lloyd, my sweet.

    LLOYD. Take the sardines off with you.

(Exit MRS. CLACKETT into study, carrying the sardines.)

    ROGER. I'm sorry about this.

    VICKI. That's all right. We don't want the television, do we?

    ROGER. Only she's been in the family for generations.

    VICKI. Great. Come on, then. *(She starts upstairs.)* I've got to be in Basingstoke by four.

    ROGER. Perhaps we should just have a glass of champagne.

    VICKI. We'll take it up with us.

    ROGER. Yes. Well ...

    VICKI. And don't let my files out of sight.

    ROGER. No. Only ...

    VICKI. What?

    ROGER. Well ...

    VICKI. Her?

    ROGER. She *has* been in the family for generations.

(Enter MRS. CLACKETT from the study, with the newspaper but without the sardines.)

    MRS. CLACKETT. Sardines ... Sardines ... It's not for me to say, of course, dear, only I will just say this: don't think twice about it — take the plunge. You'll really enjoy it here.

    VICKI. Oh. Great.

    MRS. CLACKETT. *(To ROGER.)* Won't she, love?

ROGER. Yes. Well. Yes!

MRS. CLACKETT. *(To VICKI.)* And we'll enjoy having you. *(To ROGER.)* Won't we, love?

ROGER. Oh. Well.

VICKI. Terrific.

MRS. CLACKETT. Sardines, sardines. Can't put your feet up on an empty stomach, can you.

(Exit MRS. CLACKETT to service quarters.)

VICKI. You see? She thinks it's great. She's even making us sardines!

ROGER. Well...

VICKI. I think she's terrific.

ROGER. Terrific.

VICKI. So which way?

ROGER. *(Picking up the bags.)* All right. Before she comes back with the sardines.

VICKI. Up here?

ROGER. Yes, yes.

VICKI. In here?

ROGER. Yes, yes, yes.

(Exeunt ROGER and VICKI into mezzanine bathroom.)

VICKI. *(Off.)* It's another bathroom.

(They reappear.)

ROGER. No, no, no.

VICKI. Always trying to get me into bathrooms.

ROGER. I mean in *here.*

(He nods at the next door — the first along the gallery. VICKI leads the way in. ROGER follows.)

VICKI. Oh, black sheets! *(She produces one.)*

ROGER. It's the airing cupboard *(He throws the sheet back.)* This one, this one.

(He drops the bag and box and struggles nervously to open the second door along the gallery, the bedroom.)

VICKI. Oh, you're in a real state! You can't even get the door open.

(Exeunt ROGER and VICKI into the bedroom. Only they can't, because the bedroom door won't open.
The sound of a key in the lock, and the front door opens. On the doorstep stands PHILIP, carrying a cardboard box. He is in his forties, with a deep suntan, and writes attractive new plays with a charming period atmosphere.)

PHILIP. ... No, it's Mrs. Clackett's afternoon off, remember.
LLOYD. Hold it.

(Enter FLAVIA carrying a flight bag like GARRY's. She is in her thirties, the perfect companion piece to the above.)

LLOYD. Hold it.
PHILIP. We've got the place entirely to ourselves.

(PHILIP closes the door. Only the door won't stay closed. A pause, while GARRY struggles to open the door upstairs, and FREDERICK struggles to close the door downstairs.)

LLOYD. And God said, 'Hold it.' And they held it. And God saw that it was terrible.
GARRY. *(To FREDERICK and BELINDA, the actor and actress playing PHILIP and FLAVIA.)* Sorry, loves, this door won't open.
BELINDA. Sorry, love, this door won't close.
LLOYD. And God said, 'Poppy!'
FREDERICK. Sorry, everyone. Am I doing something wrong? You know how stupid I am about doors.

BELINDA. Freddie, my sweet, you're doing it perfectly.
FREDERICK. As long as it's not me that's broken it.

(Enter POPPY from the wings.)

LLOYD. And there was Poppy. And God said, 'Be fruitful and multiply, and fetch Tim to fix the doors.'

(Exit POPPY into the wings.)

BELINDA. Oh, I love technicals!
GARRY. She loves technicals! *(Fondly.)* Isn't she just, I mean, honestly, she loves technicals! Dotty! Where's Dotty?
BELINDA. Everyone's always so nice to everyone.
GARRY. Oh! Isn't she just, I mean, she really is, isn't she. *(Enter DOTTY from the service quarters. To DOTTY.)* Belinda's being all, you know.
BELINDA. But Freddie, my precious, don't *you* like a nice all-night technical?
FREDERICK. The only thing I like about technicals is you get a chance to sit on the furniture. *(He sits.)*
BELINDA. Oh, Freddie, my precious! It's lovely to see you cheering up and making jokes. *(She sits beside him, and embraces him.)*
FREDERICK. Oh, was that a joke?
BELINDA. This is such a lovely company to work with. It's such a happy company.
DOTTY. Wait till we've got to Stockton-on-Tees in twelve weeks time.
BELINDA. Are you all right, Lloyd, my precious?
LLOYD. I'm starting to know what God felt like when he sat out there in the darkness creating the world. *(He takes a pill.)*
BELINDA. What did he feel like, Lloyd, my love?
LLOYD. Very pleased he'd taken his Valium.
BELINDA. He had six days, of course. We've only got six hours.
LLOYD. And God said, 'Where the fuck is Tim?' *(Enter from the wings TIM, the company stage manager. He is exhausted.)* And

there the fuck *was* Tim. And God said, 'Let there be doors, that open when they open, and close when they close.'

TIM. Do something?

LLOYD. Doors.

TIM. I was doing the front of house.

LLOYD. Doors.

TIM. Doors?

LLOYD. Tim, are you fully awake?

BELINDA. Lloyd, he *has* been putting the set up all weekend.

LLOYD. You're not trying to do too much, are you, Tim?

BELINDA. Tim, my love, this door won't close.

GARRY. And the bedroom won't, you know.

TIM. Oh, right.

(He sets to work on the doors.)

BELINDA. *(To LLOYD.)* He hasn't been to bed for forty-eight hours.

LLOYD. Don't worry, Tim. Only another twenty-four hours, and it'll be the end of the day.

(LLOYD comes up on stage.)

BELINDA. Oh, look, he's come down to earth amongst us.

LLOYD. Listen. Since we've stopped anyway. OK, it took two days to get the set up, so we shan't have time for a dress rehearsal. Don't worry. Think of the first night as a dress rehearsal. If we can just get through the play once tonight for doors and sardines. That's what it's all about. Doors and sardines. Getting on — getting off. Getting the sardines on — getting the sardines off. That's farce. That's the theatre. That's life.

BELINDA. Oh, Lloyd, you're so deep.

LLOYD. So just keep going. Bang, bang, bang. Bang you're on. Bang you've said it. Bang you're off. And everything will be perfectly where's Selsdon?

BELINDA. Oh no!

GARRY. Not already?

BELINDA. Selsdon!

GARRY. Selsdon!

LLOYD. Poppy!

DOTTY. *(To LLOYD.)* I thought he was in front, with you?

LLOYD. I thought he was round the back, with you? *(Enter POPPY from the wings.)* Is Mr. Mowbray in his dressing room?

(Exit POPPY into the wings.)

FREDERICK. Oh, I don't think he would. Not at a technical. *(To BROOKE.)* Would he?

BROOKE. Would who?

GARRY. Selsdon. We can't find him!

FREDERICK. I'm sure he wouldn't. Not at a technical.

DOTTY. Half a chance, he would.

BROOKE. Would what?

(GARRY, DOTTY and LLOYD make gestures to her of tipping a glass, or raising the elbow, or screwing the nose.)

BELINDA. Now come on, my sweets, be fair! We don't know.

FREDERICK. Let's not jump to any conclusions.

LLOYD. Let's just get the understudy dressed. Tim!

TIM. Yes?

LLOYD. Hurry up with those doors. You're going on as the Burglar.

TIM. Oh. Right.

DOTTY. He shouldn't have been out of sight! I said, he must never be out of sight!

BELINDA. He's been as good as gold all the way through rehearsals.

GARRY. Yes, because in the rehearsal room it was all, I don't know, but there we were, do you know what I mean?

LLOYD. There was no set. You could see everyone.

GARRY. And here it's all, you know.

LLOYD. Split into two. There's a front and a back. And instantly we've lost him.

(*Enter POPPY from the wings.*)

POPPY. He's not in the dressing room.

DOTTY. You've looked in the lavatories?

POPPY. Yes.

DOTTY. And the scenery dock and the prop room and the paint store?

POPPY. Yes.

FREDERICK. (*To DOTTY.*) You've worked with him before, of course.

LLOYD. (*To POPPY.*) Ring the police. (*Exit POPPY into the wings. To TIM.*) Finished the doors? Right, get the Burglar gear on. (*Exit TIM into the wings. Enter SELSDON MOWBRAY from the back of the stalls. He is in his seventies, and is wearing his BURGLAR gear. He comes down the aisle during the following dialogue, and stands in front of the stage, watching everyone on it.*) I'm sorry, Dotty, my love.

DOTTY. No, it's my fault, Lloyd, my love.

LLOYD. I cast him.

DOTTY. 'Let's give him one last chance,' I said. 'One last chance!' I mean, what can you do? We were in weekly rep together in Peebles.

GARRY. (*To DOTTY.*) It's my fault, my precious. I shouldn't have let you. This tour for her isn't just, do you know what I mean? This is her life savings!

LLOYD. We know that, Garry, love.

(*BELINDA puts a hand on DOTTY's arm.*)

DOTTY. I'm not trying to make my fortune.

FREDERICK. Of course you're not, Dotty.

DOTTY. I just wanted to put a little something by.

BELINDA. We know, love.

GARRY. Just something to buy a little house that she could I mean, come on, that's not so much to ask.

(*BROOKE puts a hand to her eye.*)

BELINDA. *(To BROOKE.)* Don't *you* cry, my sweet! It's not *your* fault!

BROOKE. No, I've got something behind my lens.

FREDERICK. Yes, you couldn't expect Brooke to keep anyone in sight.

DOTTY. *(Pointing at SELSDON without seeing him.)* But he was standing right there in the stalls before we started! I saw him!

BROOKE. Who are we talking about now?

BELINDA. It's all right, my sweet. We know you can't see anything.

BROOKE. You mean *Selsdon?* I'm not *blind.* I can see *Selsdon.*

(They all turn and see him.)

BELINDA. Selsdon!

GARRY. Oh my God, he's here all the time!

LLOYD. Standing there like Hamlet's father.

FREDERICK. My word, Selsdon, you gave us a surprise. We thought you were... We thought you were... not there.

DOTTY. Where have you been, Selsdon?

BELINDA. Are you all right, Selsdon?

LLOYD. Speak to us!

SELSDON. Is it a party?

BELINDA. 'Is it a party?'!

SELSDON. Is it? How killing! I got it into my head there was going to be a rehearsal. *(He goes up on to the stage.)* I was having a little postprandial snooze at the back of the stalls so as to be ready for the rehearsal.

BELINDA. Isn't he lovely?

LLOYD. Much lovelier now we can see him.

SELSDON. So what are we celebrating?

BELINDA. 'What are we celebrating?'!

(Enter TIM from the wings.)

TIM. I've looked all through his dressing room. I've looked all through the wardrobe. I can't find the gear. *(LLOYD indicates*

SELSDON.) Oh.

SELSDON. Beer? In the wardrobe?

LLOYD. No, Selsdon. Tim, you need a break. Why don't you sit down quietly upstairs and do all the company's VAT?

TIM. VAT, right.

LLOYD. *(Discreetly.)* And Tim — just in case he and the gear *do* walk off together one night, order yourself a spare Burglar costume.

TIM. Spare Burglar costume.

LLOYD. *Two* spare Burglar costumes. One to fit you, one to fit Poppy. I want a plentiful supply of spare Burglars on hand for any eventuality.

TIM. Two spare Burglars.

(Exit TIM into the wings.)

BELINDA. He has been on his feet for forty-eight hours, Lloyd.

LLOYD. *(Calling.)* Don't fall down, Tim. We may not be insured.

SELSDON. So what's next on the bill?

LLOYD. Well, Selsdon, I thought we might try a spot of rehearsal.

SELSDON. Oh, I won't, thank you.

LLOYD. You *won't?*

SELSDON. You all go ahead. I'll sit and watch you. This is the beer in the wardrobe, is it?

BELINDA. No, my sweet, he wants us to rehearse.

SELSDON. Yes, but I think we've got to rehearse, haven't we?

LLOYD. Rehearse, yes! Well done, Selsdon. I knew you'd think of something. Right, from Belinda and Freddie's entrance...

(Enter POPPY from the wings, alarmed.)

POPPY. Lloyd...

LLOYD. What? What's happened now?

POPPY. The police!

LLOYD. The *police?*

POPPY. They've found an old man. He was lying unconscious in a doorway just across the street.

LLOYD. Oh. Yes. Thank you.

POPPY. They say he's very dirty and rather smelly, and I thought oh my God, because...

LLOYD. Thank you, Poppy.

POPPY. Because when you get close to Selsdon...

BELINDA. POPPY!

POPPY. No, I mean, if you stand anywhere near Selsdon you can't help noticing this very distinctive...

(She stops, sniffing.)

SELSDON. *(Putting his arm round her.)* I'll tell you something, Poppy. Once you've got it in your nostrils you never forget it. Sixty years now and the smell of the theatre still haunts me.

(Exit SELSDON into the study.)

BELINDA. Oh, bless him!

LLOYD. Tell me, Poppy, love — how did you get a job like this, that requires tact and understanding? You're not somebody's girlfriend, are you?

(POPPY gives him a startled look.)

BELINDA. Don't worry, Poppy, my sweet. He truly did not hear.

(Enter SELSDON from the study.)

SELSDON. *Not* here?

LLOYD. Yes, yes, there!

BELINDA. Sit down, my precious.

DOTTY. Go back to sleep.

LLOYD. You're not on for another twenty pages yet.

(Exit SELSDON into the study. Exit POPPY into the wings.)

LLOYD. And on we go. *(He goes back down into the auditorium.)* Dotty in the kitchen, wildly roasting sardines. Freddie and Belinda waiting impatiently outside the front door. Garry and Brooke disappearing tremulously into the bedroom. Time sliding irrevocably into the past.

(Exeunt DOTTY into the service quarters, GARRY and BROOKE upstairs into the bedroom, and FREDERICK through the front door.)

BELINDA. *(To LLOYD, with lowered voice.)* Aren't they sweet?
LLOYD. What?
BELINDA. *(Points to the bedroom and the service quarters.)* Garry and Dotty.
LLOYD. Garry and Dotty?
BELINDA. Sh!
LLOYD. *(Lowers his voice.)* What? You mean they're an item? Those two? Tramplemain and Mrs. Clackett?
BELINDA. It's supposed to be a secret.
LLOYD. But she's old enough to be...
BELINDA. Sh! Didn't you know?
LLOYD. I'm just God, Belinda, love. I'm just the one with the English degree, I don't know anything.

(Enter GARRY from the bedroom.)

GARRY. What's happening?
LLOYD. I don't like to imagine, Garry, honey.

(Exit BELINDA through the front door.)

GARRY. I mean, what are we waiting for?

(Enter DOTTY from the service quarters, inquiringly.)

LLOYD. I don't know what you're waiting for, Garry. Her sixteenth birthday?

GARRY. What?

LLOYD. Or maybe just the cue. Brooke! *(Exit DOTTY to the service quarters. Enter BROOKE from the bedroom.)* 'Oh, you're in a real state.'

VICKI. Oh, you're in a real state! You can't even get the door open.

LLOYD. Door closed, love.

(GARRY closes the door.)

VICKI. You can't even get the door open.

(Exeunt ROGER and VICKI into the bedroom. Enter PHILIP through the front door.)

PHILIP. No, it's Mrs. Clackett's afternoon off, remember. *(Enter FLAVIA carrying a flight bag like GARRY's.)* We've got the place entirely to ourselves.

(PHILIP closes the door.)

FLAVIA. Home!

PHILIP. Home, sweet home!

FLAVIA. Dear old house!

PHILIP. Just waiting for us to come back!

FLAVIA. It's rather funny, though, creeping in like this for our wedding anniversary!

PHILIP. It's damned serious! If Inland Revenue finds out we're in the country, even for one night, bang goes our claim to be resident abroad. Bang goes most of this year's income. I feel like an illegal immigrant.

FLAVIA. I'll tell you what I feel like.

PHILIP. Champagne? *(He takes a bottle out of the box.)*

FLAVIA. I wonder if Mrs. Clackett's aired the beds.

PHILIP. Darling!

FLAVIA. Well, why not? No children. No friends dropping in. We're absolutely on our own.

PHILIP. True. *(He picks up the bag and box and ushers FLAVIA towards the stairs.)* There is something to be said for being a tax exile.
FLAVIA. Leave those!

(He drops the bag and box and kisses her. She flees upstairs, laughing, and he after her.)

PHILIP. Sh!
FLAVIA. What?
PHILIP. *(Humorously.)* Inland Revenue may hear us!

(They creep to the bedroom door.
Enter MRS. CLACKETT from the service quarters carrying a fresh plate of sardines.)

MRS. CLACKETT. *(To herself.)* What I did with that first lot of sardines I shall never know.

(She puts the sardines on the telephone table and sits on the sofa.)

PHILIP and FLAVIA. *(Looking down from the gallery.)* Mrs. Clackett!

(MRS. CLACKETT jumps up.)

MRS. CLACKETT. Oh, you give me a turn! My heart jumped right out of my boots!
PHILIP. So did mine!
FLAVIA. We thought you'd gone!
MRS. CLACKETT. I thought you was in Spain!
PHILIP. We are! We are!
FLAVIA. You haven't seen us!
PHILIP. We're not here!
MRS. CLACKETT. Oh, like that, is it? The income tax are after you?
FLAVIA. They would be, if they knew we were here.
MRS. CLACKETT. All right, then, love. You're not here. I have-

n't seen you. Anybody asks for you, I don't know nothing. Off to bed, are you?

PHILIP. Oh...

FLAVIA. Well...

MRS. CLACKETT. That's right. Nowhere like bed when they all get on top of you. You'll want your things, look. *(She indicates the bag and box.)*

PHILIP. Oh. Yes. Thanks.

(He comes downstairs, and picks up the bag and box.)

MRS. CLACKETT. *(To FLAVIA.)* Oh, and that bed hasn't been aired, love.

FLAVIA. I'll get a hot water bottle.

(Exit FLAVIA into the mezzanine bathroom.)

MRS. CLACKETT. I've put all your letters in the study, dear.

PHILIP. Letters? What letters? You forward all the mail, don't you?

MRS. CLACKETT. Not the ones from the income tax, dear. I don't want to spoil your holidays.

PHILIP. Oh good heavens! Where are they?

MRS. CLACKETT. I've put them all in the pigeonhouse.

PHILIP. In the *pigeonhouse*?

MRS. CLACKETT. In the little pigeonhouse in your desk, love.

(Exeunt MRS. CLACKETT and PHILIP into the study. PHILIP is still holding the bag and box. Only he remains on, and DOTTY remains in the doorway waiting for him.
Enter ROGER from the bedroom, still dressed, tying his tie.)

ROGER. Yes, but I could hear voices!

(Enter VICKI from the bedroom in her underwear.)

VICKI. Voices? What sort of voices?

LLOYD. Hold it. Freddie, what's the trouble?

FREDERICK. Lloyd, you know how stupid I am about moves. Sorry, Garry. ... Sorry, Brooke. ... It's just my usual dimness. *(To LLOYD.)* But why do I take the things off into the study? Wouldn't it be more natural if I left them on?

LLOYD. No.

FREDERICK. I thought it might be somehow more logical.

LLOYD. No.

FREDERICK. Lloyd, I know it's a bit late in the day to go into all this...

LLOYD. Freddie, we've got several more minutes left before we open.

(Enter BELINDA from the mezzanine bathroom, to wait patiently.)

FREDERICK. Thank you, Lloyd. As long as we're not too pushed. But I've never understood why he carries an overnight bag and a box of groceries into the study to look at his mail.

GARRY. Because they have to be out of the way for my next scene!

FREDERICK. I see that.

BELINDA. And Freddie, my sweet, Selsdon needs them in the study for *his* scene.

FREDERICK. I see that...

LLOYD. *(Comes up on stage.)* Selsdon ... where is he? Is he there?

BELINDA. *(Calling, urgently.)* Selsdon!

DOTTY. *(Likewise.)* Selsdon!

GARRY. *(Likewise.)* Selsdon!

(A pane of glass shatters in the mullion window, and an arm comes through and releases the catch. Enter an elderly BURGLAR. He has great character, but is in need of extensive repair and modernization.)

BURGLAR. No bars, no burglar alarm. They ought to be prosecuted for incitement... *(He becomes aware of the others.)* No?

LLOYD. No. Not yet. Thank you, Selsdon.

SELSDON. I thought I heard my name.

LLOYD. No, no, no. Back to sleep, Selsdon. Another ten pages before the big moment.

SELSDON. I'm so sorry.

LLOYD. Not at all. Nice to see you. Poppy, put the glass back in the window. *(Enter POPPY. She puts the glass back.)* And, Selsdon....

SELSDON. Yes?

LLOYD. Beautiful performance.

SELSDON. Oh, how kind of you. I don't think I'm quite there yet, though.

(Exit SELSDON through the window.)

LLOYD. He even remembered the line.

FREDERICK. All right, I see all that.

LLOYD. *(Faintly.)* Oh, no!

FREDERICK. I just don't know why I take them.

LLOYD. Freddie, love, why does anyone do anything? Why does that other idiot walk out through the front door holding two plates of sardines? *(To GARRY.)* I'm not getting at you, love.

GARRY. Of course not, love. *(To FREDERICK.)* I mean, why do I? *(To LLOYD.)* I mean, right, when you come to think about it, why *do* I?

LLOYD. Who knows? The wellsprings of human action are deep and cloudy. *(To FREDERICK.)* Maybe something happened to you as a very small child which made you frightened to let go of groceries.

BELINDA. Or it could be genetic.

GARRY. Yes, or it could be, you know.

LLOYD. It could well be.

FREDERICK. Of course. Thank you. I understand all that. But...

LLOYD. Freddie, love, I'm telling you — I don't know. I don't think the author knows. I don't know why the author came into this industry in the first place. I don't know why any of us came into it.

FREDERICK. All the same, if you could just give me a reason I could keep in my mind...

LLOYD. All right, I'll give you a reason. You carry those groceries into the study, Freddie, honey, because it's just slightly after midnight, and we're not going to be finished before we open tomorrow night. Correction — before we open *tonight. (FREDERICK nods, rebuked, and exits into the study. DOTTY silently follows him. GARRY and BROOKE go silently back into the bedroom. LLOYD returns to the stalls.)* And on we go. From after Freddie's exit, *with* the groceries.

BELINDA. *(Keeping her voice down.)* Lloyd, sweetheart, his wife left him this morning.

LLOYD. Oh. *(Pause.)* Freddie! *(Enter FREDERICK, still wounded, from the study.)* I think the point is that you've had a great fright when she mentions income tax, and you feel very insecure and exposed, and you want something familiar to hold on to.

FREDERICK. *(With humble gratitude.)* Thank you, Lloyd. *(He clutches the groceries to his chest.)* That's most helpful.

(Exit FREDERICK into the study.)

BELINDA. *(To LLOYD.)* Bless you, my sweet.

LLOYD. *(Leaves the stage.)* And on we merrily go. *(Exit BELINDA into the mezzanine bathroom.)* 'Yes, but I could hear voices...'

(Enter ROGER from the bedroom, still dressed, tying his tie.)

ROGER. Yes, but I could hear voices!

(Enter VICKI from the bedroom in her underwear.)

VICKI. Voices? What sort of voices?

ROGER. People's voices.

VICKI. But there's no one here.

ROGER. Darling, I saw the door-handle move! It could be someone from the office, checking up.

VICKI. I still don't see why you've got to put your tie on to look.

ROGER. Mrs. Crackett.

VICKI. Mrs. Crackett?

ROGER. One has to set an example to the staff.

VICKI. *(Looks over the banisters.)* Oh, look, she's opened our sardines.

(She moves to go downstairs. ROGER grabs her.)

    ROGER. Come back!
    VICKI. What?
    ROGER. I'll fetch them! You can't go downstairs like that.
    VICKI. Why not?
    ROGER. Mrs. Crackett.
    VICKI. Mrs. Crackett?
    ROGER. One has certain obligations.

(Enter MRS. CLACKETT from the study. She is carrying the first plate of sardines.)

MRS. CLACKETT. *(To herself.)* Sardines here. Sardines there. It's like a Sunday school outing. *(ROGER pushes VICKI through the first available door, which happens to be the linen cupboard.)* Oh, you're still poking around, are you?

ROGER. Yes, still poking ... well, still around.

MRS. CLACKETT. In the airing cupboard, were you?

ROGER. No, no. *(The linen cupboard door begins to open. He slams it shut.)* Well, just checking the sheets and pillowcases. Going through the inventory. *(He starts downstairs.)* Mrs. Blackett...

MRS. CLACKETT. Clackett, dear, Clackett.

(She puts down the sardines beside the other sardines.)

ROGER. Mrs. Clackett. Is there anyone else in the house, Mrs. Clackett?

MRS. CLACKETT. I haven't seen no one, dear.

ROGER. I thought I heard voices.

MRS. CLACKETT. Voices? There's no voices here, love.

ROGER. I must have imagined it.

PHILIP. *(Off.)* Oh good Lord above!

(ROGER, with his back to her, picks up both plates of sardines.)

ROGER. I beg your pardon?
MRS. CLACKETT. Oh good Lord above, the study door's open.

(She crosses and closes it. ROGER looks out of the window.)

ROGER. There's another car outside! That's not Mr. Hackham's, is it? Or Mr. Dudley's?

(Exit ROGER through the front door, holding both plates of sardines. Enter FLAVIA from the mezzanine bathroom, carrying a hot water bottle. She sees the linen cupboard door swinging open as she passes, pushes it shut, and turns the key.)

FLAVIA. Nothing but flapping doors in this house.

(Exit FLAVIA into the bedroom
(Enter from the study PHILIP, holding a tax demand and its envelope.)

PHILIP. '... final notice... steps will be taken... distraint... proceedings in court...'
MRS. CLACKETT. Oh yes, and that reminds me, a gentleman come about the house.
PHILIP. Don't tell me. I'm not here.
MRS. CLACKETT. He says he's got a lady quite aroused.
PHILIP. Leave everything to Squire, Squire, Hackham and Dudley.
MRS. CLACKETT. All right, love. I'll let them go all over, shall I?
PHILIP. Let them do anything. Just so long as you don't tell anyone we're here.
MRS. CLACKETT. So I'll just sit down and turn on the... sardines, I've forgotten the sardines! I don't know — if it wasn't fixed to my shoulders I'd forget what day it was.

(Exit MRS. CLACKETT to the service quarters.)

PHILIP. I didn't get this! I'm not here. I'm in Spain. But if I didn't get it I didn't open it.

(Enter FLAVIA from the bedroom. She is holding the dress that VICKI arrived in.)

FLAVIA. Darling, I never had a dress like this, did I?
PHILIP. *(Abstracted.)* Didn't you?
FLAVIA. I shouldn't buy anything as tarty as this... Oh, it's not something you gave me, is it?
PHILIP. I should never have touched it.
FLAVIA. No, it's lovely.
PHILIP. Stick it down. Put it back. Never saw it.

(Exit PHILIP into study.)

FLAVIA. Well, I'll put it in the attic, with all the other things you gave me that are too precious to wear.

*(Exit FLAVIA along the upstairs corridor.
Enter ROGER through the front door, still carrying both plates of sardines.)*

ROGER. All right, all right... Now the study door's open again! What's going on? *(He puts the sardines down — one plate on the telephone table, where it was before, one near the front door — and goes towards the study, but stops at the sound of urgent knocking overhead.)* Knocking! *(Knocking.)* Upstairs! *(He runs upstairs. Knocking.)* Oh my God, there's something in the airing cupboard! *(He unlocks it and opens it. Enter VICKI.)* Oh, it's you.
VICKI. Of course it's me! You put me in here! In the dark! With all black sheets and things!
ROGER. But, darling, why did you lock the door?
VICKI. Why did *I* lock the door? Why did *you* lock the door!
ROGER. *I* didn't lock the door!
VICKI. *Someone* locked the door!
ROGER. Anyway, we can't stand here like this.

VICKI. Like what?
ROGER. In your underwear.
VICKI. OK, I'll take it off.
ROGER. In here, in here!

(He ushers her into the bedroom.
Only she remains on, blinking anxiously, and peering about the floor.
GARRY waits for her, holding the bedroom door open.
Enter PHILIP from the study, holding the tax demand, the envelope,
and a tube of glue.)

PHILIP. Darling, this glue. Is it the sort you can never get un-
stuck...?
LLOYD. Hold it.
PHILIP. Oh, Mrs. Clackett's made us some sardines.
LLOYD. Hold it. We have a problem.
FREDERICK. *(To BROOKE.)* Oh, bad luck! Which one is it this
time?
BROOKE. Left.
GARRY. *(Calling to people, off.)* It's the left one, everybody!
OMNES. *(Off.)* Left one!

(Enter DOTTY, BELINDA, and POPPY.)

FREDERICK. It could be anywhere.
GARRY. *(Looks over the edge of the gallery.)* It could have gone
over the thing and fallen down, you know, and then bounced somewhere else again.

(BROOKE comes downstairs. They all search hopelessly.)

POPPY. Where did you last see it?
BELINDA. She *didn't* see it, poor sweet! It was in her eye!
GARRY. *(Coming downstairs.)* It was probably on 'Why did I
lock the door?' She opens her eyes very sort of, you know. Don't you,
my sweet? I always feel I ought to rush forward and — *(He rushes
forward, hands held out.)*

DOTTY. Mind where you put your feet, my love.

FREDERICK. Yes, everyone look under their feet.

GARRY. No one move their feet.

BELINDA. Everyone put their feet back exactly where they were.

FREDERICK. Pick your feet up one by one.

(They all trample about, looking under their feet, except BROOKE, who crouches with her good eye at floor level. LLOYD comes up on stage.)

LLOYD. Brooke, love, is this going to happen during a performance? We don't want the audience to miss their last buses and trains.

BELINDA. She'll just carry on. Won't you, my love?

FREDERICK. But can she see anything without them?

LLOYD. Can she hear anything without them?

BROOKE. *(Suddenly realizing that she is being addressed.)* Sorry?

(She straightens up sharply. Her head comes into abrupt contact with POPPY's face.)

POPPY. Ugh!

BROOKE. Oh. Sorry.

(BROOKE jumps up to see what damage she has done to POPPY, and steps backward on to GARRY's hand.)

GARRY. Ugh!

BROOKE. Sorry.

(DOTTY hurries to his aid.)

DOTTY. Oh my poor darling! *(To BROOKE.)* You stood on his hand!

FREDERICK. Oh dear. (*He hurriedly clasps a handkerchief to his nose.*)

BELINDA. Oh, look at Freddie, the poor love!

LLOYD. What's the matter with *him*?

BELINDA. He's just got a little nosebleed, my sweet.

LLOYD. A nosebleed? No one touched him!

BELINDA. No, he's got a thing about violence. It always makes his nose bleed.

FREDERICK. *(From behind his handkerchief.)* I'm so sorry.

LLOYD. Brooke, sweetheart...

BROOKE. I thought you said something to me.

LLOYD. Yes. *(He picks up a vase and hands it to her.)* Just go and hit the box-office manager with this, and you'll have finished off live theatre in Weston-super-Mare.

BROOKE. Anyway, I've found it.

BELINDA. She's found it!

DOTTY. Where was it, love?

BROOKE. In my eye.

GARRY. In her eye!

BELINDA. *(Hugging her.)* Well done, my sweet.

LLOYD. Not in your left eye?

BROOKE. It had gone round the side.

BELINDA. I knew it hadn't gone far. Are you all right, Poppy, my sweet?

POPPY. I think so.

BELINDA. Freddie?

FREDERICK. Fine, fine. *(He gets to his feet, looks in his hand-kerchief, and has to sit down again.)* I'm so sorry.

LLOYD. *Now* what?

BELINDA. He's just feeling a little faint, my love. He's got this thing about... *(She tries to demonstrate.)*

LLOYD. This thing about what?

BELINDA. Well, I won't say the word.

(FREDERICK gets to his feet.)

LLOYD. You mean blood?

FREDERICK. Oh dear. *(He has to sit down again.)*

BELINDA. *(To FREDERICK.)* We all understand, my precious.

LLOYD. All right, clear the stage. Walking wounded carry the stretcher cases. *(LLOYD returns to the stalls, DOTTY to the service quarters, POPPY to the wings. GARRY and BROOKE go upstairs. BELINDA helps FREDERICK to his feet.)* Right, then. On we bloodily stagger. *(FREDERICK has to reach for a chair again.)* Oh, sorry, Freddie. Let me rephrase that. On we blindly stumble. Brooke, I withdraw that. *(Exit BELINDA along the upstairs corridor, FREDERICK into study.)* From your exit, anyway. 'OK, I'll take it off.... In here, in here.' Where's Selsdon?

    GARRY. Selsdon!
    LLOYD. Selsdon!

(Enter SELSDON through the front door.)

    SELSDON. I think she might have dropped it out here somewhere.

    LLOYD. Good. Keep looking. Only another five pages, Selsdon. *(Exit SELSDON through the front door.)* 'Anyway, we can't stand here like this. — Like what?. — In your underwear. — OK, I'll take it off.'

    ROGER. In here, in here!

(He ushers her into the bedroom.
Enter PHILIP from the study, holding the tax demand, the envelope,
    and a tube of glue.)

    PHILIP. Darling, this glue. Is it the sort you can never get unstuck...? Oh, Mrs. Clackett's made us some sardines.

(Exit PHILIP into the study with the tax demand, envelope, glue and
    one of the plates of sardines from the telephone table.
Enter ROGER from the bedroom, holding the hot water bottle. He
    looks up and down the landing.
Enter VICKI from the bedroom.)

    VICKI. Now what?
    ROGER. A hot water bottle! *I* didn't put it there!
    VICKI. *I* didn't put it there.
    ROGER. Someone in the bathroom, filling hot water bottles.

(Exit ROGER into the mezzanine bathroom.)

    VICKI. *(Anxious.)* You don't think there's something creepy going on?

(Exit VICKI into the mezzanine bathroom.
Enter FLAVIA along the upstairs corridor.)

    FLAVIA. Darling, are you coming to bed or aren't you?

(Exit FLAVIA into the bedroom.
Enter ROGER and VICKI from the mezzanine bathroom.)

    ROGER. What did you say?
    VICKI. I didn't say anything.
    ROGER. I mean, first the door handle. Now the hot water bottle...
    VICKI. I can feel goose-pimples all over.
    ROGER. Yes, quick, get something round you.
    VICKI. Get the covers over our heads.

(ROGER is about to open the bedroom door.)

    ROGER. Just a moment. What did I do with those sardines? *(He goes downstairs. VICKI makes to follow.)* You — wait here.
    VICKI. *(Uneasily.)* You hear all sorts of funny things about these old houses.
    ROGER. Yes, but this one has been extensively modernized throughout. I can't see how anything creepy would survive oil-fired central heating and...
    VICKI. What? What is it?

(ROGER stares at the telephone table in silence
The bedroom door opens, and FLAVIA puts ROGER's flight bag on
*   the table outside without looking round. The door closes*
*   again.)*

    VICKI. What's happening?

ROGER. The sardines. They've gone.
VICKI. Perhaps there is something funny going on. I'm going to get into bed and put my head under the...

(She freezes at the sight of the flight bag.)

ROGER. I put them there. Or was it *there?*
VICKI. Bag ....

(VICKI runs down the stairs to ROGER, who is directly underneath the gallery.)

ROGER. I suppose Mrs. Sprockett must have taken them away again... What? What is it?
VICKI. Bag!
ROGER. Bag?
VICKI. Bag! Bag!

(VICKI drags ROGER silently back towards the stairs.
Enter FLAVIA from the bedroom with the box of files. She picks up the flight bag as well, and takes them both off along the upstairs corridor.)

ROGER. What do you mean, bag, bag?
VICKI. Bag! Bag! Bag!
ROGER. What bag?

(VICKI sees the empty table outside the bedroom door.)

VICKI. No bag!
ROGER. No bag?
VICKI. Your bag! Suddenly! Here! Now — gone!
ROGER. It's in the bedroom. I put it in the bedroom.

(Exit ROGER into the bedroom.)

VICKI. Don't go in there!

(Enter ROGER from the bedroom.)

ROGER. The box!
VICKI. The box!
ROGER. They've both gone!
VICKI. Oh! My files!
ROGER. What on earth's happening? Where's Mrs. Spratchett?
(He starts downstairs. VICKI follows him.) You wait in the bedroom.
VICKI. No! No! No!

(She runs downstairs.)

ROGER. At least put your dress on!
VICKI. I'm not going in there!
ROGER. I'll fetch it for you, I'll fetch it for you!

(Exit ROGER into the bedroom.)

VICKI. Yes, quick — let's get out of here!

(Enter ROGER from the bedroom.)

ROGER. Your dress has gone.
VICKI. I'm never going to see Basingstoke again!

(ROGER goes downstairs.)

ROGER. Don't panic! Don't panic! There's some perfectly rational explanation for all this. I'll fetch Mrs. Splotchett and she'll tell us what's happening. You wait here... You can't stand here looking like that... Wait in the study... Study, study, study!

(Exit ROGER into the service quarters.
VICKI opens the study door. There's a roar of exasperation from PHILIP, off. She turns and flees.)

VICKI. Roger! There's a strange figure in there! Where are you?

(There is another cry from PHILIP, off.
Exit VICKI blindly through the front door.
Enter PHILIP from the study. He is holding the tax demand in his
right hand, and one of the plates of sardines in his left.)

PHILIP. Darling, I know this is going to sound silly, but...

(He struggles to get the tax demand unstuck from his fingers, encum-
bered by the plate of sardines.
Enter FLAVIA along the upstairs corridor, carrying various pieces of
bric-a-brac.)

FLAVIA. Darling, if we're not going to bed I'm going to clear
out the attic.
PHILIP. I can't come to bed! I'm glued to a tax demand!
FLAVIA. Darling, why don't you put the sardines down?

(PHILIP puts the plate of sardines down on the table. But when he
takes his hand away the sardines come with it.)

PHILIP. Darling, I'm stuck to the sardines!
FLAVIA. Darling, don't play the fool. Get that bottle marked
poison in the downstairs loo. That eats through anything.

(Exit FLAVIA along the upstairs corridor.)

PHILIP. *(Flapping the tax demand.)* I've heard of people getting
stuck with a problem, but this is ridiculous.

(Exit PHILIP into the downstairs bathroom.
Pause.)

LLOYD. Selsdon...? You're on, Selsdon. We're there. The moment's arrived...
BELINDA. *(Off.)* It's all right, love. He's coming, he's coming...
LLOYD. But his arm should be coming through that window
even before Freddie's off!

(A pane of glass shatters in the mullion window, and an arm comes through and releases the catch.)

LLOYD. Ah. And here it is.

(The window opens, and through it appears an elderly BURGLAR. He has great character, but is in need of extensive repair and modernization.)

BURGLAR. No bars, no burglar alarm. They ought to be prosecuted for incitement.

(He climbs in.)

LLOYD. All right, Selsdon, hold it. Let's take it again.
BURGLAR. No, but sometimes it makes me want to sit down and weep. When I think I used to do banks! When I remember I used to do bullion vaults!
LLOYD. Hold it, Selsdon. Hold it!
BURGLAR. What am I doing now?
LLOYD. *Hold it!*

(Enter POPPY from the wings.)

BURGLAR. I'm breaking into paper bags!
POPPY. Lloyd wants you to hold it.

(Enter BELINDA.)

BURGLAR. Right, what are they offering... ?
BELINDA. Stop, Selsdon, my love! Wait, my precious!

(SELSDON stops, restrained at last by BELINDA's hand on his arm.)

LLOYD. It's like Myra Hess playing on through the air raids.
SELSDON. Stop?
POPPY. Stop.

BELINDA. Stop.

LLOYD. Thank you, Belinda. Thank you, Poppy. *(Exeunt BELINDA and POPPY.)* Selsdon...

SELSDON. I met Myra Hess once.

LLOYD. I think he can hear better than I can.

SELSDON. I beg your pardon?

LLOYD. From your entrance, please, Selsdon.

SELSDON. Well, it was during the war, at a charity show in Sunderland...

LLOYD. Thank you! Poppy!

SELSDON. Oh, not for me. It stops me sleeping.

(Enter POPPY from the wings.)

LLOYD. Put the glass back once more.

SELSDON. Come on again?

LLOYD. Right. Only, Selsdon...

SELSDON. Yes?

LLOYD. A little sooner, Selsdon. A shade earlier. A touch closer to yesterday. All right? Freddie! *(Enter FREDERICK. To SELSDON.)* Start moving as soon as Freddie opens the door. *(To FREDERICK.)* What's the line?

FREDERICK. 'I've heard of people getting *stuck* with a problem, but this is ridiculous.'

LLOYD. Start moving as soon as you hear the line, 'I've heard of people getting stuck with a *problem*...'

FREDERICK. 'Stuck with a *problem*'?

LLOYD. 'Stuck with a *problem*, but this is ridiculous.' And I want your arm through that window. Right?

SELSDON. Say no more. May I make a suggestion, though? Should I perhaps come on a little earlier?

LLOYD. Selsdon...

SELSDON. Only there does seem to be something of a hiatus between Freddie's exit and my entrance.

LLOYD. No, Selsdon. Listen. Don't worry. I've got it.

SELSDON. Yes?

LLOYD. How about coming on a little earlier?

SELSDON. We're obviously thinking along the same lines.

(Exit SELSDON through the window.)

LLOYD. Am I putting him on or is he putting me on? Right,
Freddie, from your exit.
PHILIP. *(Flapping the tax demand.)* I've heard of people getting
stuck with a *problem*, but this is ridiculous.

*(Exit PHILIP into downstairs bathroom.
Enter BURGLAR as before, but on time.)*

BURGLAR. No bars, no burglar alarms. They ought to be prosecuted for incitement. *(He climbs in.)* No, but sometimes it makes me
want to sit down and weep. When I think I used to do banks! When I
remember I used to do bullion vaults! What am I doing now? I'm
breaking into paper bags! So what are they offering? *(He peers at the
television.)* One microwave oven. *(He unplugs it and puts it on the
sofa.)* What? Fifty quid? Hardly worth lifting it. *(He inspects the
paintings and ornaments.)* Junk ... Junk... If you insist... *(He pockets
some small item.)* Where's his desk? No, they all say the same thing...
They all say the same thing...
SELSDON. Yes? Line?
POPPY. *(Off.)* 'It's hard to adjust to retirement.'
SELSDON. What?
LLOYD. *(Wearily.)* 'It's hard to adjust to retirement.'
SELSDON. Hard to what?
OTHERS. *(Variously, off.)* 'Adjust to retirement.'
SELSDON. It's also very hard to hear if everyone talks at once.

*(Exit BURGLAR into the study.
Enter ROGER from the service quarters, followed by MRS. CLACK-
ETT, who is holding another plate of sardines.)*

ROGER. ... And the prospective tenant naturally wishes to know
if there is any previous history of paranormal phenomena.
MRS. CLACKETT. Oh, yes, dear, it's all nice and paranormal.

ROGER. I mean, has anything ever dematerialized before? Has anything ever...? *(He sees the television set on the sofa.)* ... flown about?

(MRS. CLACKETT puts the sardines down on the telephone table, moves the television set back, and closes the front door.)

MRS. CLACKETT. Flown about? No, the things move themselves on their own two feet, just like they do in any house.

ROGER. I'd better warn the prospective tenant. She is inspecting the study. *(He opens the study door and then closes it again.)* There's a man in there!

MRS. CLACKETT. No, no, there's no one in the house, love.

ROGER. *(Opening the study door.)* Look! Look! He's... *searching for* something.

MRS. CLACKETT. *(Glancing briefly.)* I can't see no one.

ROGER. You can't see him? But this is extraordinary! And where is my prospective tenant? I left her in there! She's gone! My prospective tenant has disappeared! *(He closes the study door, and looks round the living room. He sees the sardines on the telephone table.)* Oh my God.

MRS. CLACKETT. Now what?

ROGER. There!

MRS. CLACKETT. Where?

ROGER. The sardines!

MRS. CLACKETT. Oh, the sardines.

ROGER. You can see the sardines?

MRS. CLACKETT. I can see the sardines. *(ROGER touches them cautiously, then picks up the plate.)* I can see the way they're going, too.

ROGER. I'm not letting these sardines out of my hand. But where is my prospective tenant?

(He goes upstairs, holding the sardines.)

MRS. CLACKETT. I'm going to be opening sardines all night, in and out of here like a cuckoo on a clock.

(Exit MRS. CLACKETT into the service quarters.)

ROGER. Vicki! Vicki!

(Exit ROGER into the mezzanine bathroom.
Enter BURGLAR from the study, carrying an armful of silver cups, etc.)

BURGLAR. No, I miss the violence. I miss having other human beings around to terrify...

(He dumps the silverware on the sofa, and exits into the study.
Enter ROGER from mezzanine bathroom.)

ROGER. Where's she gone? Vicki?

(Exit ROGER into the linen cupboard.)
Enter BURGLAR from the study, carrying PHILIP's box and bag. He
*   empties the contents of the box out behind the sofa, and loads the*
*   silverware into the box.)*

BURGLAR. It's nice to hear a bit of shouting and screaming around you. All this silence gets you down...

(Enter ROGER from the linen cupboard, still holding the sardines.)

ROGER. *(Calls.)* Vicki! Vicki!

(Exit ROGER into the bedroom.)

BURGLAR. I'm going to end up talking to myself...

(Exit the BURGLAR into study, unaware of ROGER.
Enter PHILIP from the downstairs bathroom. His right hand is still
*   stuck to the tax demand, his left to the plate of sardines.)*

PHILIP. Darling, this stuff that eats through anything. It eats through *trousers!* *(He examines holes burnt in the front of them.)* Darling, if it eats through trousers, you don't think it goes on and eats through... Listen, darling, I think I'd better get these trousers off! *(He begins to do so, as best he can.)* Darling, quick, this is an emergency! I mean, if it eats through absolutely anything... Darling, I think I can feel it! I think it's eating through... absolutely everything!

(Enter ROGER from the bedroom, still holding the sardines.)

ROGER. There's something evil in this house.

(PHILIP pulls up his trousers.)

PHILIP. *(Aside.)* The Inland Revenue!
ROGER. *(Sees PHILIP, frightened.)* He's back!
PHILIP. No!
ROGER. No?
PHILIP. I'm not here.
ROGER. He's not there!
PHILIP. I'm abroad.
ROGER. He's walking abroad.
PHILIP. I must go.
ROGER. Stay!
PHILIP. I won't, thank you.
ROGER. Speak!
PHILIP. Only in the presence of my lawyer.
ROGER. Only in the presence of your...? Hold on. You're not from the other world!
PHILIP. Yes, yes — Marbella!
ROGER. You're some kind of intruder!
PHILIP. Well, nice to meet you. *(He waves goodbye with his right hand, then sees the tax demand on it, and hurriedly puts it away behind his back.)* I mean, have a sardine.

(He offers the sardines on his left hand. His trousers, unsupported, fall down.)

ROGER. No, you're not! You're some kind of sex maniac!

You've done something to Vicki! I'm going to come straight down-stairs...!

(ROGER comes downstairs and dials 999.)

PHILIP. Oh, you've got some sardines. Well, if there's nothing I can offer you...

ROGER. This is plainly a matter for the police! *(Into the phone.)* Police!

PHILIP. ... I think I'll be running along.

(He runs, his trousers still round his ankles, out through the front door.)

ROGER. Come back...! *(Into the phone.)* Hello — police? Some-one has broken into my house! Or rather someone has broken into someone's house... No, but he's a sex maniac! I left a young woman here, and what's happened to her no one knows!

(Enter VICKI through the window.)

VICKI. There's a man lurking in the undergrowth!

ROGER. *(Into the phone.)* Sorry ... the young woman has reap-peared. *(Hand over phone.)* Are you all right?

VICKI. No, he almost saw me!

ROGER. *(Into the phone.)* He almost saw her... Yes, but he's a burglar as well! He's taken our things!

VICKI. *(Finds PHILIP's bag and box.)* The things are here.

ROGER. *(Into the phone.)* The things have come back. So we're just missing a plate of sardines.

VICKI. *(Finding the sardines left near the front door by ROGER.)* Here are the sardines.

ROGER. *(Into the phone.)* And we've found the sardines.

VICKI. This is the police? You want the police here? In my un-derwear?

ROGER. *(Into the phone.)* So what am I saying? I'm saying, let's say no more about it. *(He puts the phone down.)* I thought something terrible had happened to you!

VICKI. It has! I know him!

ROGER. You know him?

VICKI. He's dealt with by our office!

ROGER. He's just an ordinary sex maniac.

VICKI. Yes, but he mustn't see me like this! You have to keep up certain standards if you work for Inland Revenue!

ROGER. Well, put something on!

VICKI. I haven't got anything!

ROGER. There must be something in the bathroom! *(He picks up the box and bag and leads the way.)* Bring the sardines!

(She picks up the sardines. Exeunt ROGER and VICKI into the downstairs bathroom.
Enter the BURGLAR from the study, and dumps more booty.)

BURGLAR. Right, that's downstairs tidied up a bit. *(He starts upstairs.)* Just give the upstairs a quick going-over for them.

(Exit the BURGLAR into the mezzanine bathroom.
Enter VICKI, holding the sardines and a white bathmat, and ROGER, carrying the box and bag, from the downstairs bathroom.)

VICKI. A *bathmat*?

ROGER. Better than nothing!

VICKI. I can't go around in front of our taxpayers wearing a *bathmat*!

ROGER. The bedroom, then! There must be something in the bedroom!

(He leads the way upstairs.)

VICKI. No, no, no, no! I'm not going in that bedroom again!

ROGER. *I'll* look in the bedroom. You look in the other bathroom.

(Exit ROGER into the bedroom and VICKI into the mezzanine bath

room.
Enter PHILIP through the front door.)

PHILIP. Darling! Help! Where are you?

(Enter VICKI from the mezzanine bathroom.)

VICKI. Roger! Roger! *(Exit PHILIP hurriedly, unseen by VICKI, into the downstairs bathroom.)* There's someone in the bathroom now!

(VICKI runs towards the bedrooms, then stops.)

FLAVIA. *(Off.)* Oh, darling, I'm finding such lovely things...! *(VICKI turns and runs downstairs instead, as FLAVIA enters along the upstairs corridor, absorbed in the china tea service she is carrying. VICKI exits hurriedly into the downstairs bathroom.)* Do you remember this china tea service — *(VICKI screams, off.)* — that you gave me on the very first anniversary of our...? *(Enter VICKI from the downstairs bathroom. She stops at the sight of FLAVIA.)* Who are you?
VICKI. Oh, *no* — it's his wife and dependents!

(She puts her hands over her face.
Enter PHILIP from the downstairs bathroom, still with his hands encumbered, holding the bathmat now as well, and keeping his trousers up with his elbows.)

PHILIP. Excuse me, I think you've dropped your dress! *(FLAVIA gasps. PHILIP looks up at the gallery and sees her. To FLAVIA.)* Where have you been? I've been going mad! Look at the state I'm in! *(He holds up his hands to show FLAVIA the state he is in, and his trousers fall down. The tea service slips from FLAVIA's horrified hands, and rains down on the floor of the living room below. PHILIP hurries towards the stairs, trousers round his ankles, his hands extended in supplication.)* Darling, honestly! *(VICKI flees before him, comes face to face with FLAVIA, and takes refuge in the linen cup-*

board.) She just burst into the room and her dress fell off!

(Exit FLAVIA, with a cry of pain, along the upstairs corridor.
Enter ROGER from the bedroom, directly in PHILIP's path. PHILIP
holds up the bathmat in front of his face. He is invisible to
ROGER, though, because the latter is holding up a white bed
sheet.)

ROGER. Here, put this sheet on for the moment while I see if
there's something in the attic.

(ROGER leaves PHILIP with the sheet and exits along upstairs corri-
dor.
PHILIP turns to go back downstairs.
Enter BURGLAR from the mezzanine bathroom, holding two gold
taps.)

BURGLAR. One pair gold taps... *(He stops at the sight of*
PHILIP.) Oh, my Gawd!
PHILIP. Who are you?
BURGLAR Me? Fixing the taps.
PHILIP. Tax? Income tax?
BURGLAR. That's right, governor. In come new taps ... out go
old taps.

(Exit BURGLAR into the mezzanine bathroom.)

PHILIP. Tax-inspectors everywhere!
ROGER. *(Off.)* Here you are!
PHILIP. The other one!

(Exit PHILIP into the bedroom, holding the bathmat in front of his
face.
Enter ROGER along the upstairs corridor holding VICKI's dress.)

ROGER. I've found your dress! It came flying out of the attic at
me!

(Exit ROGER into mezzanine bathroom.
Enter PHILIP from the bedroom, trying to pull the bathmat off his head.)

PHILIP. Darling! I've got her dress stuck to my head now!

(Enter ROGER from the mezzanine bathroom.
Exit PHILIP into the bedroom.)

ROGER. Another intruder!

(Enter the BURGLAR from the mezzanine bathroom.)

BURGLAR Just doing the taps, governor.
ROGER. Attacks? Not attacks on women?
BURGLAR. Try anything, governor, but I'll do the taps on the bath first.

(Exit BURGLAR into the mezzanine bathroom.)

ROGER. Sex maniacs everywhere! Where is Vicki? Vicki... ?

(Exit ROGER into the downstairs bathroom.
Enter BURGLAR from the mezzanine bathroom, heading for the front door.)

BURGLAR People everywhere! I'm off. A tax on women? I don't know, they'll put a tax on anything these days.

(Enter ROGER from the downstairs bathroom. The BURGLAR stops.)

ROGER. If I can't find her, you're going to be in trouble, you see.
BURGLAR. WC? I'll fix it.

(Exit BURGLAR into the mezzanine bathroom again.)

ROGER. Vicki ... ?

(Exit ROGER through the front door.
Enter PHILIP from the bedroom. The bathmat is still on his head, but
is now arranged like a burnous, and he is wrapped in a white bed
sheet.
Enter VICKI from the linen cupboard, enrobed from head to foot
in a black bed sheet. They both quietly close the doors behind
them.)

VICKI. Roger!   *(Together.)*   PHILIP. Darling!

(They see each other and start back.
Enter ROGER through the front door.)

ROGER. Sheikh! I thought you were coming at four? And this is
your charming wife? So you want to see over the house now, do you,
Sheikh? Right. Well. Since you're upstairs already...

(ROGER goes upstairs.
Enter FLAVIA along the upstairs corridor, carrying a vase.)

FLAVIA. Him and his floozie! I'll break this over their heads!
ROGER. ... let's start downstairs.

(ROGER, PHILIP and VICKI go downstairs.)

FLAVIA. Who are you? Who are these creatures?
ROGER. *(To PHILIP and VICKI.)* I'm sorry about this. I don't
know who she is. No connection with the house, I assure you. *(Enter
MRS. CLACKETT from the service quarters, with another plate of
sardines. ROGER advances to introduce her.)* Whereas this good lady
with the sardines, on the other hand...
MRS. CLACKETT. No other hands, thank you, not in my sardines, 'cause this time I'm eating them.
ROGER. ... is fully occupied with her sardines, so perhaps the
toilet facilities would be of more interest.

(He ushers PHILIP and VICKI away from MRS. CLACKETT towards the mezzanine bathroom.)

FLAVIA. Mrs. Clackett, who are these people?

MRS. CLACKETT. Oh, we get them all the time, love. They're just Arab sheets.

ROGER. I'm sorry about this. *(He opens the door to the mezzanine bathroom.)* But in here...

FLAVIA. *Arab* sheets?

(Exit FLAVIA into the bedroom.)

ROGER. In here we have...

(Enter the BURGLAR from the mezzanine bathroom.)

BURGLAR. Ballcocks, governor. Your ballcocks have gone.

ROGER. We have him.

(Enter FLAVIA from the bedroom.)

FLAVIA. They're *Irish* sheets! Irish linen sheets off my own bed!

MRS. CLACKETT. Oh, the thieving devils!

ROGER. In the *study,* however ...

MRS. CLACKETT. You give me that sheet, you devil! *(She seizes the nearest sheet, and it comes away in her hand to reveal VICKI.)* Oh, and there she stands in her smalls, for all the world to see!

ROGER. It's you!

FLAVIA. It's her!

*(FLAVIA comes downstairs menacingly.
Exit PHILIP discreetly into the study.)*

BURGLAR. It's my little girl!

VICKI. Dad!

(FLAVIA stops.

Enter PHILIP from the study in amazement. [He is now played by a double — TIM.])

BURGLAR. Our little Vicki, that ran away from home, I thought I'd never see again!

MRS. CLACKETT. Well, would you believe it?

VICKI. *(To BURGLAR.)* What are you doing here like this?

BURGLAR. What are *you* doing here like *that?*

VICKI. Me? I'm taking our files on tax evasion to Inland Revenue in Basingstoke.

PHILIP/TIM. Agh!

(He collapses behind the sofa, clutching at his heart, unnoticed by the others.)

FLAVIA. *(Threateningly.)* So where's my other sheet?

(Enter through the front door the most sought-after of all properties on the market today — a SHEIKH. He is wearing Arab robes, and bears a strong resemblance to PHILIP, since he is also played by FREDERICK.)

SHEIKH. Ah! A house of heavenly peace! I rent it!

ROGER. Hold on, hold on... I know that face! *(Pulls the SHEIKH's burnous aside to reveal his face.)* He isn't a sheikh! He's that sex-maniac!

FLAVIA. Yes — it's my husband!

SHEIKH. What?

(They all fall upon him.
FREDERICK's trousers are revealed to be around his ankles.)

LLOYD. Trousers!

MRS. CLACKETT. You take all the clean sheets! *(She tries to pull the robes off him.)*

SHEIKH. What? What?

LLOYD. Trousers! Trousers!

VICKI. You snatch my bathmat! *(She tries to pull his burnous off him.)*

SHEIKH. What? What? What?

FLAVIA. You toss me aside like a broken china doll! *(She hits him.)*

LLOYD. And to cap it all you've got your trousers on!

(Everyone except SELSDON finally comes to a halt.)

BURGLAR. And what you're up to with my little girl down there in Basingstoke...

(Even SELSDON becomes aware that the action has ceased.)

SELSDON. Stop?

BELINDA. Stop, stop.

(LLOYD comes up on stage.)

LLOYD. It's a question of authenticity, you see, Freddie. *Do* Arab potentates wear trousers under their robes? I don't know. Maybe they do. But not round their ankles, Freddie! Not round their ankles!

FREDERICK. Sorry. It's just frightfully difficult doing a quick-change without a dresser.

LLOYD. Get Tim to help you. Tim! Where's Tim? Come on, Tim! Tim!

(TIM, wearing the sheet as PHILIP's double, gets to his feet and gazes blearily at LLOYD.)

TIM. Sorry?

LLOYD. Oh, yes. You're acting.

TIM. I must have dropped off down there.

LLOYD. Never mind, Tim.

TIM. Do something?

LLOYD. No, let it pass. We'll just struggle through on our own. Tim has a sleep behind the sofa, while all the rest of us run round with our trousers round our ankles. OK, Freddie? You'll just have to do the best you can. On we go, then... *(FREDERICK hesitates.)* Some other problem, Freddie?

FREDERICK. Well, since we're stopped anyway.

LLOYD. Why did I ask?

FREDERICK. I mean, you know how stupid I am about plot.

LLOYD. I know, Freddie.

FREDERICK. May I ask another silly question?

LLOYD. All my studies in world drama lie at your disposal.

FREDERICK. I still don't understand why the Sheikh just happens to be Philip's double.

GARRY. Because he comes in and we all think he's, you know, and we all, I mean, that's the joke.

FREDERICK. I see that.

BELINDA. My sweet, the rest of the plot depends on it!

FREDERICK. I see that. But it *is* rather a coincidence, isn't it?

LLOYD. It *is* rather a coincidence, Freddie, yes. Until you reflect that there was an earlier draft of the play, now unfortunately lost to us. And in this the author makes it clear that Philip's father as a young man had traveled extensively in the Middle East.

FREDERICK. I see... I *see*!

LLOYD. You see?

FREDERICK. That's very interesting.

LLOYD. I thought you'd like that.

FREDERICK. But will the audience get it?

LLOYD. You must tell them, Freddie. Looks. Gestures. That's what acting's all about. OK?

FREDERICK. Yes. Thank you, Lloyd. Thank you.

LLOYD. And it will be even more powerful when you do it with no trousers.

FREDERICK. Of course. *(Takes his trousers off.)*

LLOYD. Right, can we just finish the act? From Belinda's beautiful line, 'You toss me aside like a broken china doll!' *(LLOYD returns to the stalls.)* I'm being so clever out here! What's going to be left of this show when I've gone off to do *Richard III* and you're up there on your own? Right — 'You toss me aside like a broken china doll!'

FLAVIA. You toss me aside like a broken china doll! *(She hits him.)*

SHEIKH. What? What? What?

BURGLAR. And what you're up to with my little girl down there in Basingstoke I won't ask. But I'll tell you one thing, Vicki.

(Pause.)

LLOYD. Brooke!

BROOKE. Sorry ...

LLOYD. Your line. Come on, love, we're two lines away from the end of the act.

BROOKE. I don't understand.

LLOYD. Give her the line!

POPPY. *(Off.)* 'What's that, Dad?'

BROOKE. Yes, but I don't understand.

BELINDA. It's 'What's that, Dad?'

SELSDON. Yes, I say to you, 'I'll tell you one thing, Vicki', and you say to me, 'What's that, Dad?'

BROOKE. I don't understand why the Sheikh looks like Philip.

(Silence. Everyone waits for the storm. LLOYD comes slowly up on stage.)

LLOYD. Poppy! Bring the book! *(Enter POPPY from the wings, with the book. Patiently.)* Is that the line, Poppy? 'I don't understand why the Sheikh looks like Philip?' Can we consult the author's text, and make absolutely sure?

POPPY. Well, I think it's ...

LLOYD. *(With exquisite politeness.)* 'What's that, Dad?' Right. That's the line, Brooke, love. We all know you've worked in very classy places up in London where they let you make the play up as you go along, but we don't want that kind of thing here, do we. Not when the author has provided us with such a considered and polished line of his own. Not at one o'clock in the morning. Not two lines away from the end of Act One. Not when we're just about to get a tea break before we all drop dead of exhaustion. We merely want to hear the line. *(Suddenly puts his mouth next to VICKI's ear and shouts.)* 'What's that, Dad?' *(All patience and politeness again.)* That's all. Nothing else. I'm not being unreasonable, am I? *(BROOKE abruptly turns, runs upstairs, and exits into the mezzanine bathroom.)* Exit? Does it say 'exit'? *(The sound of BROOKE weeping, off, and running downstairs.)* Oh dear, now she's going to wash her lenses away.

(Exit LLOYD through the front door.)

    FREDERICK. *(Chastened.)* Oh good Lord.
    SELSDON. *(Likewise.)* A little heavy with the sauce, I thought.
    GARRY. I thought it was going to be Poppy when he finally, you know.
    DOTTY. It's usually Poppy. Isn't it, love?

(POPPY smiles wanly.)

    FREDERICK. I suppose that was all my fault.
    GARRY. But why pick on, you know?
    DOTTY. Yes, why Brooke?
    BELINDA. I thought it was quite sweet, actually.
    GARRY. Sweet?
    BELINDA. Trying to pretend they're not having a little thing together.
    DOTTY. A little thing? Lloyd and Brooke... ?
    BELINDA. Didn't you know?
    SELSDON. Brooke and Lloyd?
    BELINDA. Where do you think they've been all weekend?
    FREDERICK. Good Lord. You mean, that's why he wasn't here when poor old Tim...

(He stops, conscious that TIM is behind the sofa.)

    DOTTY. ... put the set up back-to-front.
    BELINDA. Sh! Here they come!

(Enter LLOYD with his arm round BROOKE.)

LLOYD. OK. All forgotten. I was irresistible.
POPPY. I think I'm going to be sick.

(Exit POPPY into the wings.)

DOTTY. Oh, no!
LLOYD. Oh, for heaven's *sake*!

(Exit LLOYD after POPPY.)

GARRY. You mean ... ?
SELSDON. Her, too?
FREDERICK. Oh great Scott!
BELINDA. Well, that's something I *didn't* know.
BROOKE. I think I'm going to faint.
DOTTY. Yes, sit down, love!

(They sit BROOKE down.)

BELINDA. Quick — do your meditation.
SELSDON. Well, that's something *she* didn't know!
BELINDA. Hush, love.
DOTTY. Two weeks' rehearsal, that's all we've had.
FREDERICK. Whatever next?
SELSDON. *Most* exciting!
BELINDA. *(Indicating BROOKE.)* Sh!
SELSDON. Oh, yes. Sh!
DOTTY. Here he comes. *(Enter LLOYD from the wings, subdued.)* Is she all right, love?
LLOYD. She'll be all right in a minute. Something she ate, probably.
GARRY. *(Indicating BROOKE.)* Yes, this one's feeling a bit, you know.
LLOYD. I'm feeling a bit, you know, myself. I think I'm going to —
BELINDA. Which?
GARRY. *(Offering a chair.)* Faint?

BELINDA. *(Offering a vase.)* Or be sick?

LLOYD. *(Subsides on to the chair.)* — need that tea break.

DOTTY. You're certainly overdoing it at the moment, love.

LLOYD. So could we just have the last line of the act?

SELSDON. Me? Last line? Right.

BURGLAR. But I'll tell you one thing, Vicki.

VICKI. *(With a murderous look at LLOYD.)* What's that, *Dad*?

BURGLAR. When all around is strife and uncertainty, there's nothing like a...

SELSDON. ... what?

POPPY. *(Off, tearful.)* Oh... 'A good old-fashioned plate of sardines.'

SELSDON. What did she say?

BELINDA. 'A good old-fashioned plate...'

(She hands him MRS. CLACKETT's plate.)

BURGLAR. A good old-fashioned plate of...

SELSDON. ... *what*?

(POPPY runs on with the book, LLOYD jumps to his feet, TIM jumps up from behind the sofa.)

EVERYONE *(Except SELSDON.)* Sardines!

(Tableau, with raised sardines. The tableau continues.)

LLOYD. And *curtain!*

POPPY. *(Realizes, sobs.)* Oh!

(She runs hurriedly into the wings.)

CURTAIN

ACT II

The living room of the Brents' country home. Wednesday afternoon.
(Theatre Royal, Ashton-under-Lyne. Wednesday matinee, Febru-
ary 13.)
But this time we are watching the action from behind; the whole set
has been turned through 180 degrees. All the doors can be
seen — there is no masking behind them. Two stairways lead up
to the platform that gives access to the doors on the upper level.
Some of the scene inside the living room is visible through the
full-length window. There are also two doors in the backstage
fabric of the theatre: one giving access to the dressing rooms,
and the pass door into the auditorium. The usual backstage fur-
nishings, including the prompt corner and props table, chairs for
the actors, a fire-point with fire buckets and fire-axe, etc.

(TIM is walking anxiously up and down in his dinner jacket.
POPPY is speaking into the microphone in the prompt corner.)

POPPY. *(Over the tannoy.)* Act One beginners, please. Your
calls, Miss Otley, Miss Ashton, Mr. Lejeune, Mr. Fellowes, Miss
Blair. Act One beginners, please.
TIM. And maybe Act One beginners is what we'll get. What do
you think?
POPPY. *(To TIM.)* Oh, Dotty'll pull herself together now we've
called Beginners. Now she knows she's got to be on stage in five min-
utes. Won't she?
TIM. Will she?
POPPY. You know what Dotty's like.
TIM. We've only been on the road for a month! We've only got

to Ashton-under-Lyne! What's it going to be like by the time we've got to Stockton-on-Tees?

POPPY. If only she'd speak!

TIM. If only she'd unlock her dressing room door! Look, if Dotty won't go on...

POPPY. Won't go on?

TIM. If she won't.

POPPY. She will.

TIM. Of course she will.

POPPY. Won't she?

TIM. I'm sure she will. But if she *doesn't*...

POPPY. She must!

TIM. She will, she will. But if she *didn't*...

POPPY. I'd have five minutes to change. Four minutes.

TIM. If only she'd say something.

(The pass door opens cautiously, and LLOYD puts his head around. He closes it again at the sight of POPPY.)

POPPY. I'll have another go. Takes your mind off your own problems, anyway.

(Exit POPPY in the direction of the dressing rooms. LLOYD puts his head back round the door.)

LLOYD. Has she gone?

TIM. Lloyd! I didn't know you were coming today!

(LLOYD comes in. He is carrying a bottle of whisky.)

LLOYD. I wasn't. I haven't.

TIM. Anyway, thank God you're here!

LLOYD. I'm not. I'm in Aberystwyth. I'm in the middle of re-hearsing *Richard III*.

TIM. Dotty and Garry ...

LLOYD. I don't want anyone to know I'm in.

TIM. No, but Dotty and Garry ...

LLOYD. I just want two hours alone and undisturbed with Brooke in her dressing room between shows, then I'm on the 7:25 back to Wales. *(Gives TIM the whisky.)* This is for Brooke. Put it somewhere safe. Make sure Selsdon doesn't get his hands on it.

TIM. Right. They've had some kind of row...

LLOYD. Good, good. *(Takes money out of his wallet and gives it to TIM.)* There's a little flower shop across the road from the stage-door. I want you to buy me some very large and expensive-looking flowers.

TIM. Right. Now Dotty's locked herself in her dressing room...

LLOYD. Don't let Poppy see them. They're not for Poppy.

TIM. No. And she won't speak to anyone...

LLOYD. First house finishes just after five, yes? Second house starts at seven-thirty?

TIM. Lloyd, that's what I'm trying to tell you — there may not *be* a show!

LLOYD. She hasn't walked out already?

TIM. No one knows *what* she's doing! She's locked in her dressing room! She won't speak to anyone!

LLOYD. You've called Beginners?

TIM. Yes!

LLOYD. I can't play a complete love-scene from cold in five minutes. It's not dramatically possible.

TIM. She's had bust-ups with Garry before, of course.

LLOYD. Brooke's had a bust-up with Garry?

TIM. Brooke? Not Brooke — Dotty!

LLOYD. Oh, Dotty.

TIM. I mean, they had the famous bust-up the week before last, when we were playing Worksop.

LLOYD. Right, right, you told me on the phone.

TIM. She went out with this journalist bloke ...

LLOYD. Journalist — yes, yes...

TIM. But you know Garry threatened to kill him?

LLOYD. Killed him, yes, I know. Listen, don't worry about Dotty — she's got money in the show.

TIM. Yes, but now it's happened again! Two o'clock this morning I'm woken up by this great banging on my door. It's Garry. Do I know where Dotty is? She hasn't come home.

LLOYD. Tim, let me tell you something about *my* life. I have the Duke of Buckingham on the phone to me for an hour after rehearsal every evening complaining that the Duke of Gloucester is sucking boiled sweets through his speeches. The Duke of Clarence is off for the entire week doing a commercial for Madeira. Richard himself — would you believe? — Richard III? *(He demonstrates.)* — has now gone down with a back problem. I keep getting messages from Brooke about how unhappy she is here, and now she's got herself a doctor's certificate for nervous exhaustion — she's going to walk! I have no time to find or rehearse another Vicki. I have just one afternoon, while Richard is fitted for a surgical corset, to cure Brooke of nervous exhaustion, with no medical aids except a little whisky — you've got the whisky? — a few flowers — you've got the money for the flowers? — and a certain faded charm. So I haven't come to the theatre to hear about other people's problems. I've come to be taken out of myself, and preferably not put back again.

TIM. Yes, but Lloyd...

LLOYD. Have you done the front-of-house calls?

TIM. Oh, the front-of-house calls!

(TIM hurries to the microphone in the prompt corner, still holding the money and whisky.)

LLOYD. And don't let Poppy see those flowers!

(Exit LLOYD through the pass door.)

TIM. *(Into microphone.)* Ladies and gentlemen, will you please take your seats. The curtain will rise in three minutes.

(Enter POPPY from the dressing rooms.)

POPPY. We're going to be so late up!

TIM. No luck?

POPPY. Belinda's having a go. I haven't even started the front of house calls yet... Money? What's this for?

TIM. Nothing, nothing! *(He puts the money behind his back and automatically produces the whisky with the other hand.)*

POPPY. Whisky!

TIM. Oh... is it?

POPPY. Where did you find that?

TIM. Well...

POPPY. Up here? You mean Selsdon's hiding them round the stage now? *(She takes the whisky.)*

TIM. Oh...

POPPY. I'll put it in the ladies' loo. At least he won't go in there. *(Enter BELINDA from the dressing rooms.)* No?

BELINDA. You know what Dotty's like when she's like this. Freddie's trying now... *(She sees the whisky.)* Oh, no!

POPPY. He's hiding them round the stage now. *(Enter FREDERICK from the dressing rooms.)* No?

FREDERICK. No.

BELINDA. You didn't try for very long, my precious!

FREDERICK. No, well... *(He sees the whisky.)* Oh dear.

BELINDA. He's hiding them on stage now.

(Exit POPPY to the dressing rooms, holding the whisky.)

FREDERICK. No, Garry came rushing out of his dressing room in a great state. I couldn't quite understand what he was saying. I often feel with Garry that I must have missed something somewhere. You know how stupid I am about that kind of thing. But I think he was saying he wanted to kill me.

BELINDA. Oh, my poor sweet!

FREDERICK. I thought I'd better leave him to it. I don't want to make things worse. He's all right, is he?

BELINDA. Who, Garry? Anything but, by the sound of it!

FREDERICK. I mean, he's going on?

TIM. Garry? *Garry's* going on. Of course he's going on. What's all this about *Garry* not going on?

BELINDA. Yes, because if you have to go on for Garry, Poppy can't go on for Dotty, because if Poppy goes on for Dotty, you'll have to be on the book!

TIM. This is getting farcical.

BELINDA. Money.

TIM. Money?

BELINDA. You're waving money around.

TIM. Oh, that's for... Oh...!

(TIM hurriedly grabs his raincoat from a peg and exits into the dressing rooms.)

FREDERICK. She's a funny woman, you know — Dotty. So up and down. She was perfectly all right last night.

BELINDA. Last night?

FREDERICK. Yes, she took me for a drink after the show in some club she knows about.

BELINDA. She was with *you?* You were with *her?*

FREDERICK. She was being very sympathetic about all my troubles.

BELINDA. She's not going to sink her teeth into you! I won't let her!

FREDERICK. No, no, she couldn't have been nicer. In fact she came back to my digs afterwards for a cup of tea, and she told me all *her* troubles. Sat there until three o'clock this morning. I don't know *what* the landlady thought!

(Enter POPPY.)

POPPY. And another thing.

BELINDA. Nothing else, my sweet!

POPPY. Where's Selsdon?

BELINDA. It turns out that it's Freddie here who's the cause of all the... Selsdon?

POPPY. He's not in his dressing room.

BELINDA. Oh — I might have guessed!

POPPY. Oh — the front-of-house calls!

BELINDA. You do the calls. I'll took for Selsdon.

FREDERICK. What shall I do?

BELINDA. *(Firmly.)* Absolutely nothing at all.

FREDERICK. Right.
BELINDA. You've done quite enough already, my pet.

(Exit BELINDA to the dressing rooms.)

POPPY. *(Into the microphone.)* Ladies and gentlemen, will you please take your seats. The curtain will rise in three minutes.

(Enter TIM from the dressing rooms in his raincoat, carrying a large bunch of flowers.)

TIM. He wants to kill someone. *(He takes off his raincoat.)*
POPPY. *Selsdon* wants to kill someone?
TIM. Garry, Garry... Selsdon?
POPPY. We've lost him.
TIM. Oh, not again!
POPPY. Flowers!
TIM. *(Embarrassed.)* Oh... Well... They're just... You know...
POPPY. *(Taking them.)* Oh, Tim that's really sweet of you!
TIM. Oh... Well...
POPPY. *(To FREDERICK.)* Isn't that sweet of him?
FREDERICK. Very charming.

(She kisses TIM.)

POPPY. I'll just look in the pub. *(She gives the flowers to FREDERICK.)* Hold these.

(Exit POPPY to the dressing rooms.)

TIM. I'll take those. *(He takes the flowers.)* Oh, the front of house calls! Hold these. *(He gives the flowers back to FREDERICK.)*

FREDERICK. Oh, I think Poppy's done them.
TIM. She gave them two minutes, did she? I'll give them one minute. *(Into the microphone.)* Ladies and gentlemen, will you please take your seats. The curtain will rise in one minute.

(He takes the flowers from FREDERICK.)

FREDERICK. Oh dear, I think she said three minutes.

TIM. *Three* minutes? *I* said three minutes! *She* said three minutes?

FREDERICK. I think so.

TIM. Hold these. *(He gives FREDERICK the flowers. Into the microphone.)* Ladies and gentlemen, will you please take your seats. The curtain will rise in two minutes.

(Enter BELINDA from the dressing rooms, holding the bottle of whisky.)

FREDERICK. Any luck?

BELINDA. No, but I found yet another bottle.

FREDERICK. Oh dear.

TIM. Oh ...

BELINDA. Hidden in the ladies' lavatory, would you believe.

FREDERICK. Oh my Lord!

TIM. *(Takes it.)* Oxfam! I'll give it to Oxfam!

(POPPY runs in from the dressing rooms.)

POPPY. He's not in the pub...

BELINDA. *(Indicates the whisky to POPPY.)* No, he's hanging round ladies' lavatories!

TIM. I'd better get the spare gear on.

(Exit TIM to the dressing rooms with the whisky.)

POPPY. *(Into the microphone.)* Ladies and gentlemen, will you please take your seats. The curtain will rise in two minutes.

FREDERICK. Oh dear — Tim's already told them two minutes.

POPPY. He's done two minutes? *(Into the microphone.)* Ladies and gentlemen, will you please take your seats. The curtain will rise in one minute.

(Enter LLOYD through the pass door.)

LLOYD. What the fuck is going on?

BELINDA. Lloyd!

FREDERICK. Great Scott!

POPPY. I didn't know you were here!

LLOYD. I'm not here! I'm at the Aberystwyth Festival! But I can't stand out there and listen to 'two minutes... three minutes... one minute... two minutes'!

BELINDA. My sweet, we're having great dramas in the dressing rooms!

LLOYD. We're having great dramas out there! *(To POPPY.)* This is the matinee, honey! There's old-age pensioners out there! 'The curtain will rise in three minutes' — we all start for the Gents. 'The curtain will rise in one minute' — we all come running out again. We don't know which way we're going!

POPPY. Lloyd, I've got to have a talk with you.

LLOYD. *(Kissing her.)* Of course, honey, of course. Looking forward to it.

POPPY. You got my message?

LLOYD. Many, many messages.

POPPY. Why didn't you answer?

LLOYD. I did! I have! I'm here!

POPPY. Lloyd, there's something I've got to tell you.

LLOYD. Go on, then.

POPPY. Well... *(She hesitates, embarrassed because other people can hear, then tries to keep her voice down.)* I went to the doctor today...

(Enter BROOKE from the dressing rooms, with the whisky.)

BELINDA. Brooke!

(LLOYD hastily abandons POPPY.)

LLOYD. *(To POPPY.)* Later, later. All right?

(BROOKE holds up the whisky.)

BELINDA. Oh, no! Not another one!

BROOKE. In my dressing room!

BELINDA. *(She takes the whisky.)* In your *dressing room*? *(To LLOYD.)* It's getting completely out of control!

FREDERICK. *(Taking the whisky.)* I'll give it to Oxfam, with the other one.

LLOYD. *(Holds out his hand for the whisky.)* I'll do it. Thank you.

BROOKE. *(Sees him.)* Lloyd! *(Peers.)* Lloyd?

LLOYD. Got it in one. *(Kisses her.)*

BROOKE. You got my message?

LLOYD. And came running, honey, and came running.

BROOKE. Lloyd, we've got to have a talk.

LLOYD. We're *going* to have a talk, my love.

BROOKE. When?

LLOYD. Later, yes? Later. *(He goes to take the whisky from FREDERICK, but is distracted by seeing the flowers that FREDERICK is holding.)* Flowers?

FREDERICK. Oh, yes, sorry. *(He gives the flowers to POPPY.)*

POPPY. Tim bought them for me. *(She puts them on her desk in the prompt corner.)*

LLOYD. *Tim?* Bought them for *you*?

POPPY. To cheer me up. *(Anxiously.)* Lloyd...

LLOYD. Nothing more, just for the moment. Thank you. *(To FREDERICK.)* Strangle Tim for me when you see him, will you?

FREDERICK. Right.

(LLOYD goes towards the pass door.)

BELINDA. But what about Dotty?

LLOYD. I don't want to hear about Dotty.

FREDERICK. And Garry?

LLOYD. Not about Garry, either.

BELINDA. What about Selsdon?

LLOYD. Listen, I think this show is beyond the help of a director. You just do it. I'll sit out there in the dark with a bag of toffees and enjoy it. OK? 'One minute' was the last call, if your memory goes back that far.

BROOKE. Lloyd!
POPPY. Wait!

(LLOYD exits through the pass door. POPPY and BROOKE jostle to follow him.)

BROOKE. *(To POPPY.)* Excuse *me*!
POPPY. I've got to talk to him!
FREDERICK. *(Separating them.)* Girls, girls!
BROOKE. *(Indicates the dressing rooms.)* I've a good mind to put my coat on and walk out of that door right here and now.
FREDERICK. Listen, if you don't feel up to performing I'm sure Poppy would always be happy to have a bash on your behalf.
BROOKE. I *beg* your pardon?
POPPY. Honestly!
BELINDA. *(Firmly.)* Brooke, you sit down and do your medita-tion. Poppy, you go and see what's happening with Dotty and Garry. *(BROOKE reluctantly sits down on the floor. Exit POPPY to the dressing rooms.)* Freddie, my sweet precious ...
FREDERICK. Did I say something wrong?

(Enter SELSDON hurriedly through the pass door.)

SELSDON. Where's Tim?
BELINDA. Selsdon! My sweet! Where have you been?
FREDERICK. Are you all right? *(He puts out a sympathetic hand, then realizes that it contains the whisky bottle.)* Oh dear.

(He hurriedly puts it out of sight behind his back.)

BELINDA. We've been looking for you everywhere!
SELSDON. Oh, yes, everywhere. In front — manager's office — bar. Not a sign of him.
BELINDA. He's looking for you in the dressing rooms.
SELSDON. That's right! Great shindig been going on down there. I thought Tim ought to know about it.
BELINDA. My love, I think he's heard.

SELSDON. Oh, everything! Oh, he really went for her! 'I know when you've got your eye on someone!'

FREDERICK. Oh dear, Dotty's got her eye on someone, has she?

SELSDON 'I've seen you creeping off into corners with that poor halfwit.'

FREDERICK. Which poor halfwit?

BELINDA. Never mind, my love.

FREDERICK. Not *Tim*?

BELINDA. No, no, no.

FREDERICK. But who else is there? Apart from me?

(Enter POPPY from the dressing rooms.)

POPPY. I think they're coming.

BELINDA. They're coming!

FREDERICK. They're coming!

SELSDON. I knew they wouldn't.

POPPY. And you're *here!*

SELSDON. Oh, yes, every word!

POPPY. Right. *(Into the microphone.)* Ladies and gentlemen, will you please take your seats. The performance is about to begin.

(Enter TIM from the dressing rooms, in BURGLAR's costume.)

TIM. They're coming.

BELINDA. And we've found Selsdon.

TIM. *(To SELSDON.)* How did *you* get here?

SELSDON. How? Through the wall!

TIM. *(Into the microphone.)* Ladies and gentlemen, will you please take your seats.

POPPY. I've done it!

TIM. *(Into the microphone.)* The performance is about to...

POPPY. I've done it, I've done it!

TIM. *(To POPPY.)* Done it? Done 'about to begin'?

POPPY. Yes! About to begin, about to begin!

TIM. *(Into the microphone.)* ... is about to... is about to begin *at any moment.*

BELINDA. Poor Lloyd! He'll choke on his toffees.

SELSDON. No, the walls are very thin, you see. 'I'm absolutely sick to death of it,' she cries... *(Takes in what TIM is wearing.)* Am I setting a bit of a trend?

TIM. *(Realizes.)* Oh...

BELINDA. *(Quickly, snatching TIM's Burglar cap off.)* Understudy rehearsal, my love.

SELSDON. Oh, for Garry, yes — very timely. 'You try to give some poor devil a leg up,' she says.

(Enter GARRY from the dressing rooms.)

BELINDA. Garry, my sweet!

SELSDON Or she may have said, 'a leg over...' Oh, and here he is.

FREDERICK. *(To GARRY.)* Are you all right?

(FREDERICK collects the box and the flight bag from the props table, and smilingly offers them to GARRY, who snatches them angrily.)

SELSDON. What does he say?

BELINDA. He's not saying anything, Selsdon, my sweet.

SELSDON. Very sensible. Only stir it up again. 'I've seen you giving him little nods and smiles!' — that's what he kept saying.

(Enter DOTTY from the dressing rooms.)

BELINDA. Dotty, my love!

SELSDON. Oh, she's emerged, has she? Come on, old girl! You're on!

FREDERICK. Are you all right?

SELSDON. Is she all right?

(DOTTY merely sighs and smiles and gives a little squeeze of the arm to BELINDA. She takes up her place by the service quarters entrance, a tragically misunderstood woman. GARRY moves point-

edly away.)

BELINDA. *(To SELSDON.)* She's fine.
TIM. All right, everyone?
SELSDON. 'Little hugs and squeezes.'
BELINDA. Hush, love.
POPPY. Curtain up?

(Everyone looks anxiously from DOTTY to GARRY and back again. DOTTY and GARRY both ignore the looks. They stand aloof, then both at the same moment turn to check their appearance in the little mirrors fixed to the back of the set.)

FREDERICK. Look, Dotty... Look, Garry... I'm not going to make a great speech, but we *have* all got to go out there and put on a performance, and well...
BELINDA. We can't do it in silence, my loves! We're going to have to speak to each other!

(Pause. Neither GARRY nor DOTTY has apparently heard.)

DOTTY. *(Suddenly, bravely, to TIM.)* What's the house like?
BELINDA. That's the spirit!
FREDERICK. Well done, Dotty!
TIM. It's quite good. Well, for a matinee.
POPPY. There's quite a crowd at the front of the back stalls.
SELSDON. *(To POPPY.)* Come on, girl, get the tabs up! Some of those OAPs out there haven't got long to go.
POPPY. Right. Quiet, then, please...
FREDERICK. Let me just say one more word... Hold it a moment, Poppy...
SELSDON. Let *me* just say one word. Sardines!
BELINDA. Sardines!
FREDERICK. Sardines!

(BELINDA rushes to the prop table to fetch DOTTY the plate of sardines that she takes on for her first entrance.)

POPPY. *(Over tannoy.)* Standing by, please. Music cue one...

(Enter LLOYD through the pass door.)

LLOYD. *Now* what?

TIM. We're just going up.

LLOYD. We've been sitting there for an hour! They've gone quiet! They think someone's died!

FREDERICK. I'm sorry, Lloyd. It's my fault. I was just saying a few words to everyone.

LLOYD. Freddie, have you ever thought of having a brain transplant?

FREDERICK. Sorry, sorry. Wrong moment. I see that.

LLOYD. Anybody else have thoughts they feel they must communicate?

POPPY. Well, not now, of course, but ...

LLOYD. *What?*

POPPY. I mean, you know, later...

LLOYD. *(To TIM, quietly, conscious that BROOKE has stopped meditating and started watching.)* And you bought these flowers for Poppy?

TIM. No... *(Conscious that POPPY is watching)* Well... yes...

LLOYD. And you didn't buy any flowers for *me*?

TIM. No... well... no...

LLOYD. Tim, have you ever heard of such a thing as jealous rage?

TIM. Yes... well... yes...

LLOYD. Then take ten pounds of your own money, Tim, and go out to the florists and buy some flowers for *me!*

TIM. Lloyd, we're just going up! I've got to run the show!

LLOYD. Never mind the show. Concentrate on the floral arrangements. Bought them for Poppy! You two could have Freddie's old brain. You could have half each.

(Exit LLOYD through the pass door. POPPY sobs.)

FREDERICK. Oh dear.

BELINDA. Don't cry, Poppy, love.

SELSDON. Just get the old bus on the road.

POPPY. *(Over tannoy, tearfully.)* Standing by, please. Elecs stand by.

GARRY. *(To himself.)* Christ! *(He hammers his fist against the back of the set in frustration.)*

POPPY. Quiet backstage!

(She waits for GARRY to subside, then gives an involuntary noisy sob herself.)

BELINDA. Hush, love.

POPPY. *(Over tannoy, tearfully.)* Music cue one go. *(The introductory music for* Nothing On.*)* Tabs going up...

[Note: the act that follows is a somewhat condensed version of the one we saw rehearsed.]

	(As the curtain rises the telephone is ringing.)
(DOTTY makes her entrance.) ———	*(Enter from the service quarters MRS. CLACKETT, carrying a plate of sardines.)*
	MRS. CLACKETT. It's no good you going on...
(There is a sound of scattered applause.) ———————————	*(She pauses a beat to acknowledge the applause.)*
	MRS. CLACKETT. I can't open sardines and answer the phone. I've only got one pair of feet.

(A small laugh.) ———————

(SELSDON, BELINDA and FREDERICK express silent relief that the show has at last started, so all their problems are over. They subside onto the backstage chairs.)

(TIM puts his raincoat on, takes out his wallet, checks his money, and exits to the dressing rooms.)

(BELINDA points out to the others that GARRY is banging his head softly against the set again.)

(FREDERICK puts the whisky down on his chair and goes across to GARRY. BELINDA watches apprehensively as FREDERICK gives GARRY's arm a silently sympathetic squeeze, and smilingly puts his fingers to his lips to remind him to be quiet. GARRY shakes him off indignantly.)

(BELINDA hurries across to draw FREDERICK off.)

(FREDERICK cannot understand what he has done to cause offence. He demonstrates what he did by giving GARRY's arm another friendly squeeze.)

(GARRY drops his props and

(Puts the sardines down on the telephone table by the sofa and picks up the phone.)

MRS. CLACKETT. Hello... Yes, but there's no one here, love... No, Mr. Brent's not here... He lives here, yes, but he don't live here now because he lives in Spain... Mr. Philip Brent, that's right... The one who writes the plays, that's him, only now he writes them in Spain... No, she's in Spain, too, they're all in Spain, there's no one here... Am I in Spain? No, I'm not in Spain, dear. I look after the house for them, but I go home at one o'clock on Wednesday, only I've got a nice plate of sardines to put my feet up with, because it's the royal what's it called on the telly — the royal you know — where's the paper, then...

(She searches in the newspaper.)

MRS. CLACKETT. ... And if it's to do with letting the house then you'll have to ring the house-agents, because they're the agents for the house... Squire, Squire, Hackham and who's the other one... ? No, they're not in Spain, they're next to the phone in the study. Squire, Squire, Hackham, and hold on, I'll go and look.

threatens to hit FREDERICK.)

*(FREDERICK takes shelter
behind BROOKE, who is now
waiting for her entrance. GARRY
chases him round and round her.)*

*(FREDERICK hurriedly puts his
handkerchief to his nose.)*

*(BELINDA urges GARRY to the
front door for his entrance.)* ———

(BROOKE makes her entrance.) ——

*(FREDERICK looks in his hand-
kerchief, and comes over faint.)*

*(DOTTY has to put her arm round
him to help him to a chair.)*

*(As GARRY turns back to collect
the flight bag he gets a fleeting
glimpse of this.)* ————————

*(As GARRY comes through the
service quarters he takes another
look.)* ————————————

(She replaces the receiver.)

MRS. CLACKETT. Always
the same, isn't it. Soon as you take
the weight off your feet, down it
all comes on your head.

*(Exit MRS. CLACKETT into the
study, still holding the newspaper.)*

(The sound of a key in the lock.)

*(The front door opens. On the
doorstep stands ROGER, holding
a cardboard box.)*

ROGER. ... I have a housekeeper, yes, but this is her afternoon off.

*(Enter VICKI through the front
door.)*

ROGER. So we've got the
place entirely to ourselves.

*(ROGER goes back and brings in a
flight bag, and closes the front door.)*

ROGER. I'll just check.

*(He opens the door to the service
quarters. VICKI gazes round.)*

ROGER. Hello? Anyone at home?

(He stamps on FREDERICK's foot and reenters.) —————— *(ROGER closes the door.)*

(FREDERICK struggles with damaged foot and bleeding nose. DOTTY gets down on her knees to examine the foot.)

ROGER. No, there's no one here. So what do you think?

VICKI. All these doors!

(GARRY keeps appearing at the various doors, trying to see what DOTTY and FREDERICK are up to.) ——————

ROGER. Oh, only a handful, really.

(He opens the various doors one after another to demonstrate.)

(BELINDA makes things worse by trying to move DOTTY's head to a less suggestive position.)

ROGER. Study... Kitchen... And a self-contained service flat for the housekeeper.

VICKI. Terrific. And which one's the ... ?

ROGER. What?

VICKI. You know ...

ROGER. The usual offices? Through here.

(He opens the downstairs bath-room door for her.)

(GARRY comes off —————— and rushes at FREDERICK and DOTTY. BELINDA pushes him back on stage.)

VICKI. Fantastic.

(Exit VICKI into the bath-room.)

(BELINDA just manages to de-
tach DOTTY from her ministra-
tions and get her back on stage
for her entrance.) ——————— *(Enter MRS. CLACKETT from the*
study, without the newspaper.)

MRS. CLACKETT. Now I've
(BELINDA tries to explain to   lost the sardines...
FREDERICK that DOTTY has
taken a fancy to him. FREDERICK   *(Mutual surprise. ROGER closes*
can't understand a world of it.)   *the door to the bathroom, and*
slips the champagne back into the
bag.)

ROGER. I'm sorry. I thought
there was no one here.

MRS. CLACKETT. I'm not
here. I'm off, only it's the royal
you know, where they wear those
hats, and they're all covered in
(BELINDA has to break off to   fruit, and who are you?
remind BROOKE to...
ROGER. I'm from the agents.
I just dropped in to... go into a
few things.

... push the bathroom door open.) —*(The bathroom door opens.)*

ROGER. Well, to check some
of the measurements...

(ROGER closes it.)

(And again.) ——————————— *(The bathroom door opens.)*

ROGER. Do one or two odd

jobs...

(BELINDA suddenly points out that SELSDON has discovered the whisky that FREDERICK left on the chair. SELSDON opens the bottle, smells it, closes it again, and then goes off to the dressing rooms with it.)

(ROGER closes it.)

ROGER. Oh, and a client. I'm showing a prospective tenant over the house.

(The bathroom door opens.)

VICKI. What's wrong with this door?

(FREDERICK goes to run after SELSDON. BELINDA silently urges him to wait there — sit still — do absolutely nothing — while she runs after SELSDON.)

(ROGER closes it.)

ROGER. She's thinking of renting it. Her interest is definitely aroused.

(Enter VICKI from bathroom.)

(Exit BELINDA in the direction of the dressing rooms in pursuit of SELSDON.)

VICKI. That's not the bedroom.

ROGER. The bedroom? No, that's the downstairs bathroom and WC suite. And this is the housekeeper, Mrs. Crockett.

MRS. CLACKETT. Clackett, dear, Clackett. Only now I've lost the newspaper.

(DOTTY makes her exit ... ——— *(Exit MRS. CLACKETT into the puts down the sardines, shaking study, carrying the sardines.) her head with misery, and begins to weep.)*

ROGER. I'm sorry about this.

VICKI. That's all right. We don't want the television, do we?

ROGER. Only she's been in the family for generations.

(FREDERICK is very agitated by this. He takes the sardines away from DOTTY, pats her on the shoulder, gives her a handkerchief, realizes that it's not in a state to be seen, puts it hurriedly away, pushes the sardines back into her hand, and edges her towards the door.)

VICKI. Great. Come on, then. *(She starts upstairs.)* I've got to be in Basingstoke by four.

ROGER. Perhaps we should just have a glass of champagne.

VICKI. We'll take it up with us.

ROGER. Yes. Well ...

VICKI. And don't let my files out of sight.

ROGER. No. Only ...

(At the last moment DOTTY realizes she hasn't got the newspaper.)

VICKI. What?

ROGER. Well ...

(FREDERICK runs and fetches it from the props table. DOTTY realizes that she is still holding the sardines, and hurls them to FREDERICK just in time...

VICKI. Her?

ROGER. She *has* been in the family for generations.

... to make her entrance.) ——— *(Enter MRS. CLACKETT from the study, with the newspaper but without the sardines.)*

MRS. CLACKETT. Sardines ...

Sardines ... It's not for me to say, of course, dear, only I will just say this: don't think twice about it — take the plunge. You'll really enjoy it here.

(Enter BELINDA from the dressing rooms leading a bewildered SELSDON, but without the whisky.)

VICKI. Oh. Great.

(FREDERICK tells her what a terrible state DOTTY is in.)

MRS. CLACKETT. *(To VICKI.)* And we'll enjoy having you. *(To ROGER.)* Won't we, love?

ROGER. Oh. Well.

VICKI. Terrific.

MRS. CLACKETT. Sardines, sardines. Can't put your feet up on an empty stomach, can you.

(They turn to watch her anxiously as she makes her exit.) ———— *(Exit MRS. CLACKETT to service quarters.)*

VICKI. You see? She thinks it's great. She's even making us sardines!

(SELSDON seizes the opportunity to depart again to the dressing rooms.)

ROGER. Well...

VICKI. I think she's terrific.

ROGER. Terrific.

(BELINDA runs after SELSDON. FREDERICK goes to run after her, but turns anxiously back to reassure DOTTY.)

VICKI. So which way?

ROGER. *(Picking up the*

(But DOTTY is now smiling bravely, and telling FREDERICK that she has pulled herself together, thanks to him.)

(DOTTY gives FREDERICK a kiss to express her gratitude.)

(As GARRY comes through the door ————————— of the mezzanine bathroom he catches a fleeting glimpse of the kiss.)

(FREDERICK takes the cardboard box and goes to make his entrance, then turns back to pick up the flight bag and looks round for BELINDA to give it to. No BELINDA. He urgently shows DOTTY the flight bag and explains the situation to her.)

(GARRY appears in the linen cupboard doorway. ————— He takes a good look at the earnest colloquy between FREDERICK and DOTTY.)

(GARRY takes the sheet from VICKI.) ————————————

bags.) All right. Before she comes back with the sardines.

VICKI. Up here?

ROGER. Yes, yes.

VICKI. In here?

ROGER. Yes, yes, yes.

(Exeunt ROGER and VICKI into mezzanine bathroom.)

VICKI. *(Off.)* It's another bathroom.

(They reappear.)

ROGER. No, no, no.

VICKI. Always trying to get me into bathrooms.

ROGER. I mean in *here*.

(He nods at the next door — the first along the gallery. VICKI leads the way in.)

(ROGER follows.)

VICKI. Oh, black sheets!

(She produces one.)

ROGER. It's the airing cupboard ...

(GARRY hurls the sheet at FRE-DERICK and DOTTY. ———— ... This one, this one.
He goes back on stage.)

(He drops the bag and box and struggles nervously to open the second door along the gallery, the bedroom.)

(DOTTY starts to run off to get BELINDA, but has to run back to help FREDERICK.)

VICKI. Oh, you're in a real state! You can't even get the door open.

(Exeunt ROGER and VICKI into the bedroom.)

(The sound of a key in the lock, and the front door opens. On the doorstep stands PHILIP, carrying a cardboard box.)

(BELINDA runs in from the dressing room, holding the bottle of whisky.

She grabs the flight bag, just manages to give the whisky to DOTTY, and...

PHILIP. ... No, it's Mrs. Clackett's afternoon off, remember.

... make her entrance.) ———— *(Enter FLAVIA carrying a flight bag like GARRY's.)*

FLAVIA. Home!

(Enter SELSDON from the dressing rooms. He asks DOTTY for the whisky.

PHILIP. Home, sweet home!

FLAVIA. Dear old house!

But DOTTY is distracted by GARRY, who silently but force-

PHILIP. Just waiting for us to come back!

*fully explains to her that he will
no longer tolerate these furtive
meetings with FREDERICK.)*

*(SELSDON tries urgently to
get the whisky off GARRY and
DOTTY as they quarrel.)*

*(GARRY and DOTTY both turn
on him in fury.)*

*(GARRY pleads with DOTTY —
kneels — weeps — hangs on to
her plate of sardines.)*

*(DOTTY breaks away from
GARRY and goes to make her entrance. SELSDON points out that
she is still holding the whisky.*

*GARRY takes it off her as she
makes her entrance.)* ————

*(SELSDON tries to get the
whisky off GARRY, but GARRY
turns to ascend the platform for
his entrance.)*

FLAVIA. It's rather funny,
though, creeping in like this for
our wedding anniversary!

*(PHILIP picks up the bag and box
and ushers FLAVIA towards the
stairs.)*

PHILIP. There is something to
be said for being a tax exile.

FLAVIA. Leave those!

*(He drops the bag and box and
kisses her. She flees upstairs,
laughing, and he after her.)*

PHILIP. Sh!

FLAVIA. What?

PHILIP. Inland Revenue may
hear us!

(They creep to the bedroom door.)

*(Enter MRS. CLACKETT from
the service quarters carrying a
fresh plate of sardines.)*

MRS. CLACKETT. *(To
herself.)* What I did with that first
lot of sardines I shall never know.

*(She puts the sardines on the
telephone table and sits on the
sofa.)*

(GARRY looks around for something to do with the whisky, and gives it to BROOKE.

BROOKE peers at it, no idea what she's supposed to do with it.

She puts it down on the steps, right in front of SELSDON, in order to undress for her entrance. While her back is turned SELSDON snatches it up and conceals it.)

PHILIP and FLAVIA.
(Looking down from the gallery.)
Mrs. Clackett!

(MRS. CLACKETT jumps up.)

MRS. CLACKETT. Oh, you give me a turn! My heart jumped right out of my boots!

PHILIP. So did mine!

FLAVIA. We thought you'd gone!

MRS. CLACKETT. I thought you was in Spain!

PHILIP. We are! We are!

(SELSDON demonstrates to BROOKE pulling a chain. BROOKE peers uncomprehendingly.)

FLAVIA. You haven't seen us!

PHILIP. We're not here!

MRS. CLACKETT. You'll want your things, look. *(She indicates the bag and box.)*

PHILIP. Oh. Yes. Thanks.

(Exit SELSDON to the dressing rooms with the whisky.)

(He comes downstairs, and picks up the bag and box.)

MRS. CLACKETT. *(To FLAVIA.)* Oh, and that bed hasn't been aired, love.

FLAVIA. I'll get a hot water bottle.

(BELINDA makes her exit.) ——— *(Exit FLAVIA into the mezzanine bathroom.)*

(BELINDA looks urgently round for SELSDON, then makes drinking gestures interrogatively to BROOKE. BROOKE points towards the dressing rooms and repeats SELSDON's incomprehensible gesture of pulling a chain. Exit BELINDA towards the dressing room.)

MRS. CLACKETT. I've put all your letters in the study, dear.

PHILIP. Oh good heavens. Where are they?

MRS. CLACKETT. I've put them all in the pigeonhouse.

(GARRY, still on the platform, tries to see what DOTTY and FREDERICK are doing, but is fetched back by BROOKE...)

PHILIP. In the pigeonhouse?

MRS. CLACKETT. In the little pigeonhouse in your desk, love.

(Exeunt MRS. CLACKETT and PHILIP into the study. PHILIP is still holding the bag and box... for his entrance.) ——————— *(Enter ROGER from the bedroom, still dressed, tying his tie.)*

ROGER. Yes, but I could hear voices!

(Enter VICKI from the bedroom in her underwear.)

(BELINDA enters urgently and signals the information that SELSDON is drinking in the lavatory.)

VICKI. Voices? What sort of voices?

(FREDERICK runs to the dressing rooms exit to deal with this,

ROGER. People's voices.

but is brought back by BELINDA and forced to sit down.)

VICKI. *(Looks over the bannisters.)* Oh, look, she's opened our sardines.

(She moves to go downstairs. ROGER grabs her.)

(DOTTY and BELINDA run towards the dressing rooms instead, but DOTTY immediately has to run back to the study door to go on. BELINDA runs back to the props table for the sardines, gives them to DOTTY, just in time for her...

ROGER. Come back!

VICKI. What?

ROGER. I'll fetch them! You can't go downstairs like that.

VICKI. Why not?

ROGER. Mrs. Crackett.

VICKI. Mrs. Crackett?

ROGER. One has certain obligations.

... to make her entrance.) ——— *(Enter MRS. CLACKETT from the study. She is carrying the first plate of sardines.)*

MRS. CLACKETT. *(To herself.)* Sardines here. Sardines there. It's like a Sunday school outing.

(BROOKE makes her exit.) ——— *(ROGER pushes VICKI through the first available door, which happens to be the linen cupboard.)*

(BELINDA tries to demonstrate to BROOKE that she is going to

MRS. CLACKETT. Oh, you're

look for SELSDON, then runs back to remind her...

still poking around, are you?

ROGER. Yes, still poking ... well, still around.

MRS. CLACKETT. In the airing cupboard, were you?

ROGER. No no.

... to open the linen cupboard door.) ———————— *(The linen cupboard door begins to open. He slams it shut.)*

ROGER. Well, just checking the sheets and pillow cases. Going through the inventory.

(Enter TIM from the dressing rooms with a second, smaller, bunch of flowers. He takes his raincoat off.)

(He starts downstairs.)

ROGER. Mrs. Blackett...

(BELINDA gestures hastily to TIM in passing to explain the situation, and exits to the dressing rooms.)

MRS. CLACKETT. Clackett, dear, Clackett.

(She puts down the sardines beside the other sardines.)

(TIM asks FREDERICK where she is going.)

ROGER. Mrs. Clackett. Is there anyone else in the house, Mrs. Clackett?

(FREDERICK demonstrates raising the elbow.)

MRS. CLACKETT. I haven't seen no one, dear.

(Enter BELINDA from the dressing rooms. She demonstrates that SELSDON has locked himself in somewhere.)

ROGER. I thought I heard voices.

MRS. CLACKETT. Voices? There's no voices here, love.

ROGER. I must have imagined it.

(PHILIP breaks off from the conversation to say ——————

————PHILIP. *(Off)* Oh good Lord above!

(TIM hands BELINDA the flowers, and dashes out to the dressing rooms.)

(ROGER, with his back to her, picks up both plates of sardines.)

(BELINDA gives the flowers to FREDERICK and fetches the fireman's axe from the fire point. She demonstrates using it to break a door down.)

ROGER. I beg your pardon?

MRS. CLACKETT. Oh good Lord above, the study door's open.

(BELINDA is going to rush off to the dressing rooms with the axe when POPPY reminds her that she has an entrance coming up. BELINDA runs up on to the platform, finds that she is still holding the axe, and gives it to BROOKE.)

(She crosses and closes it. ROGER looks out of the window.)

ROGER. There's another car outside! That's not Mr. Hackham's, is it? Or Mr. Dudley's?

(Exit ROGER through the front door, holding both plates of sardines.)

(But before BELINDA can explain what to do with the axe, she has to make her entrance.) ——

(GARRY advances threateningly upon FREDERICK and points suspiciously at the flowers he is holding.)

(Enter FLAVIA from the mezzanine bathroom, carrying a hot water bottle. She sees the linen cupboard door swinging open as she passes, pushes it shut, and turns the key.)

FLAVIA. Nothing but flapping

doors in this house.

(FREDERICK has to hand GARRY the flowers in order to make his entrance.) ——————

(Exit FLAVIA into the bedroom.)

(Enter from the study PHILIP, holding a tax demand and its envelope.)

(BROOKE comes down from the platform and asks GARRY what she is supposed to do with the axe. GARRY takes it thoughtfully and puts the flowers into her hands. BELINDA, coming down from the platform to go off after SELSDON, stops at the sight of GARRY with the axe, as he looks at it and feels the edge. He looks at the door through which FREDERICK will exit. BELINDA looks at the door likewise. GARRY looks back at the axe. BELINDA looks back at the axe. GARRY begins to smile an evil smile. Horrified, BELINDA quickly takes the flowers from BROOKE and sends her off in her place to find SELSDON, then tries to get the axe away from GARRY. GARRY holds it behind his back. BELINDA, still holding the flowers, puts her arms round GARRY, trying to reach the axe.)

PHILIP. ' ... final notice... steps will be taken... distraint... proceedings in court...'

MRS. CLACKETT. Oh yes, and that reminds me, a gentleman come about the house.

PHILIP. Don't tell me. I'm not here.

MRS. CLACKETT. So I'll just sit down and turn on the... sardines, I've forgotten the sardines! I don't know — if it wasn't fixed to my shoulders I'd forget what day it was.

(DOTTY appears ——————— *just in time to see BELINDA with her arms round GARRY.)*

(Exit MRS. CLACKETT to the service quarters.)

(POPPY urges BELINDA upstairs

PHILIP. I didn't get this! I'm not here. I'm in Spain. But if I

for her entrance. BELINDA flees
up to the platform and opens the
door to make her entrance. ———

She makes one desperate effort to
grab the dress from the backstage
hook where it is hanging, then
gives up, and enters still carrying
the flowers instead. —————

BELINDA, on stage, has to vary
the line.) ————————

(DOTTY launches herself upon
GARRY. He produces the axe in
explanation of his behavior.
DOTTY snatches it from him,
and raises it to hit him.)

(FREDERICK appears —————
and snatches the axe from
DOTTY, in the nick of time. He
innocently gives it to GARRY,
who raises it to hit FREDERICK.
DOTTY snatches it from GARRY,

didn't get it I didn't open it.

(Enter FLAVIA from the bedroom.

She is holding flowers instead of
the dress that VICKI arrived in.)

FLAVIA. Darling, I never had
a dress...
... or rather a bunch of flowers
like this, did I?

PHILIP. *(Abstracted.)* Didn't
you?

FLAVIA. I shouldn't buy
anything as tarty as this... Oh, it's
not something you gave me, is it?

PHILIP. I should never have
touched it.

FLAVIA. No, it's lovely.

PHILIP. Stick it down. Put it
back. Never saw it.

(Exit PHILIP into study.)

FLAVIA. Well, I'll put it in
the attic, with all the other things
you gave me that are too precious
to wear.

and raises it once again to hit him.

BELINDA appears ———————— (Exit FLAVIA along the upstairs and snatches the axe from corridor.) DOTTY...

... as GARRY makes his entrance.) — (Enter ROGER through the front door, still carrying both plates of sardines.)

ROGER. All right, all right...
(Enter TIM from the dressing Now the study door's open again!
rooms. He grabs the axe from What's going on?
BELINDA and returns to the
dressing rooms.) (He puts the sardines down — one plate on the telephone table,
(BELINDA is going to follow him, where it was before, one near the but then realizes that there is... front door — and goes towards the study.)

*... no knocking ———————————ROGER. Knocking!
because BROOKE is still off.)*

(GARRY on stage repeats the line.) ———————————————ROGER. Knocking...!
Knocking...? Upstairs! *(He runs*
*(BELINDA realizes what's upstairs.)
wrong, and knocks on the set
with a prop.) ——————————(Knocking.)*

ROGER. Oh my God, there's something in the airing cupboard!

(He unlocks it and opens it.
(BROOKE doesn't make her
entrance ——————————— Looks for VICKI.)

*because she is still off in the
dressing rooms.)*

*(GARRY comes through the
linen cupboard door to look for
BROOKE. He improvises.)* ————

*(BELINDA tells POPPY to read in
BROOKE's part from the book.)*

*(BELINDA hands the flowers to
FREDERICK and runs off to the
dressing rooms, still holding the
axe.)*

ROGER. Oh, it's you.

————ROGER. Is it you...? I mean,
you know, hidden under all the
sheets and towels in here... I can't
just stand here and, you know,
indefinitely ...

POPPY. *(Reading.)* Of course
it's me! You put me in here! In
the dark! With all black sheets
and things!

————————ROGER. But, darling, why did
you lock the door?

VICKI. Why did *I* lock the
door? Why did *you* lock the door!

————————ROGER. I didn't lock the
door!

*(Enter LLOYD like a whirlwind
through the pass door. He de-
mands silently to know what's
going on. FREDERICK tries to
explain, while POPPY and
GARRY continue to play the
scene.)*

VICKI. *Someone* locked the
door!

————————ROGER. Anyway, we can't
stand here like this.

*(FREDERICK hands LLOYD
the flowers to make ready for
his entrance.)*

VICKI. Like what?

ROGER. In your underwear.

VICKI. OK, I'll take it off.

ROGER. In here, in here!

(LLOYD shoves the flowers into DOTTY's hands to get rid of them, and indicates to the terrified POPPY that she is to go on for BROOKE.)

(Exit ROGER into the bedroom.)

(Enter PHILIP from the study, holding the tax demand, the envelope, and a tube of glue.)

(Enter BELINDA from the dressing rooms with BROOKE, just in time for her to see LLOYD tearing POPPY's skirt off.)

PHILIP. Darling, this glue. Is it the sort that you can never get unstuck ... ? Oh, Mrs. Clackett's made us some sardines.

(Exit PHILIP into the study with the tax demand, envelope, glue and one of the plates of sardines from the telephone table.)

(GARRY stands half on and half off, waiting for BROOKE. At the sight of BROOKE, LLOYD abandons POPPY, and instead urges BROOKE upstairs for the next scene, for which she is now late.)

(Enter ROGER from the bedroom, holding the hot water bottle. He looks up and down the landing.)

ROGER. A hot water bottle! I didn't put it there!

(GARRY improvises.)

I didn't put this hot water bottle. I mean, you know, I'm standing out here, with the hot water bottle in my hands...

(BROOKE makes her entrance through the linen cupboard door... ... and starts to play the previous scene that she missed.)

VICKI. Of course it's me! You put me in here! In the dark! With all black sheets and things!

(LLOYD despairs at BROOKE's inflexibility. DOTTY asks LLOYD if the flowers are really for her.

ROGER. Someone in the bath-

He pushes them back to her absently. DOTTY is very touched. She gives him a grateful kiss...

... just as GARRY appears to see it.)

room, filling hot water bottles... What?

(Exit ROGER into the mezzanine bathroom.)

VICKI. Why did *I* lock the door? Why did *you* lock the door!

(GARRY moves closer to see, and cuts three pages of script.

ROGER. *(Off.)* Don't panic! Don't panic!

He panics, and stands for a moment unable to think where he is or what he is doing, then enters through the airing cupboard instead of the bedroom.)

(Enter ROGER, and goes downstairs.)

(Everyone backstage panics as well: 'Where are we?')

ROGER. There's some perfectly rational explanation for all this. I'll fetch Mrs. Splotchett and she'll tell us what's happening. You wait here... You can't stand here looking like that ... Wait in the study... Study, study, study!

(POPPY desperately turns over the pages of the book to find the new place, while everyone else looks over her shoulder.)

(Enter TIM from the dressing rooms, leading SELSDON, who is holding his trousers up. TIM is holding the whisky, and the axe embedded in a shattered section of the door of the Gents. He hands the whisky to FREDERICK.)

(Exit ROGER into the service quarters.)

(VICKI opens the study door. There's a roar of exasperation

(FREDERICK roars

and goes to make his entrance, then realizes that he is holding the whisky instead of his props.

FREDERICK gives a cry of alarm, claps his hand over his mouth, then realizes he was suppose to give a cry anyway, drops the whisky under the chairs, grabs his props, and...
... makes his entrance. ————

(TIM gives the axe to LLOYD and snatches the flowers from DOTTY, who snatches them right back, leaving TIM with only one. He hands this to LLOYD, who hands it to BROOKE. She peers at it as it keels sadly over, then hurls it on to the floor and runs out to the dressing rooms.)

(LLOYD gives more money to TIM, who puts his raincoat on and exits wearily to the dressing rooms.)

from PHILIP off. She turns and flees.)

VICKI. Roger! There's a strange figure in there! Where are you?

(There is another cry from PHILIP, off.)

(Exit VICKI blindly through the front door.)

(Enter PHILIP from the study. He is holding the tax demand in his right hand, and one of the plates of sardines in his left.)

PHILIP. Darling, I know this is going to sound silly, but ...

(He struggles to get the tax demand unstuck from his fingers, encumbered by the plate of sardines.)

(Enter FLAVIA along the upstairs corridor, carrying various pieces of bric-a-brac.)

FLAVIA. Darling, if we're not going to bed I'm going to clear out the attic.

PHILIP. I can't come to bed! I'm glued to a tax demand!

FLAVIA. Darling, why don't you put the sardines down?

(PHILIP puts the plate of sardines down on the table. But when he takes his hand away the sardines come with it.)

(SELSDON explains to everyone where he innocently was by a show of pulling a chain. The demonstration causes his trousers to fall down. SELSDON stoops to retrieve his fallen trousers, and sees the whisky that FREDERICK concealed beneath the chairs. He picks it up, and LLOYD snatches it out of his hand.)

PHILIP. Darling, I'm stuck to the sardines!

FLAVIA. Darling, don't play the fool. Get that bottle marked poison in the downstairs loo. That eats through anything.

(Exit FLAVIA along the upstairs corridor.)

PHILIP. *(Flapping the tax demand.)* I've heard of people getting stuck with a problem, but this is ridiculous.

(FREDERICK exits ——————— and sees that SELSDON is otherwise occupied.)

(Exit PHILIP into the downstairs bathroom.)

(FREDERICK repeats the cue ——— and slams the door again.)

PHILIP. But this is ridiculous.

(They all suddenly realize that this is SELSDON's cue. They rush him to the window. He raises his arms to open the window and his trousers fall down.

(Exit PHILIP into the downstairs bathroom.)

*They bundle him on as best they
can.)* ─────────────── *(The window opens, and through
it appears an elderly BURGLAR.)*

*(They watch him. Then GARRY
snatches the flowers from
DOTTY, and hurls them on the
floor. FREDERICK reproachfully
picks them up, and hands them
back to DOTTY.)*

BURGLAR No bars, no
burglar alarm. They ought to be
prosecuted for incitement.

(He climbs in.)

BURGLAR. No, but some-
times it makes me want to sit
down and weep. When I think I
used to do banks! When I
remember I used to do bullion
vaults! What am I doing now? I'm
breaking into paper bags! So what
are they offering? *(He peers at the
television.)* One microwave oven.

*(GARRY grabs the axe from
LLOYD and advances upon
FREDERICK. DOTTY hands the
flowers to BELINDA so as to be
able to throw her arms protec-
tively round FREDERICK.
BELINDA dumps the flowers on
POPPY's desk so as to be able
to snatch FREDERICK away
from DOTTY. DOTTY snatches
him back. They snatch him back
and forth, like two dogs with a
bone, then push him aside and
face up to each other. DOTTY
grabs the axe from GARRY to
use on BELINDA. But they are
distracted because...*

(He unplugs it and puts it on the sofa.)

BURGLAR. What? Fifty quid?
Hardly worth lifting it.

*(He inspects the paintings and
ornaments.)*

BURGLAR. Junk ... Junk ... if
you insist...

(He pockets some small item.)

BURGLAR. Where's his desk?
No, they all say the same thing...

*SELSDON appears at the front
door.)* ─────────────── *(He opens the front door to get a*

prompt.)

SELSDON. Yes? Yes? 'They all say the same thing...?'

POPPY. 'It's hard to adjust to retirement.'

SELSDON. Hard to what?

OMNES. *(Shouting.)* 'Adjust to retirement!'

(SELSDON goes back on.) ———— BURGLAR. It's hard to assess a requirement.

(SELSDON makes his exit.) ——— *(Exit BURGLAR into the study.)*

(DOTTY is about to resume her attack upon BELINDA when she realizes that GARRY is already making his entrance.) ———— *(Enter ROGER from the service quarters.)*

ROGER. ... And the prospective tenant naturally wishes to know if there is any previous history of paranormal phenomena.

(DOTTY hands the axe panic-stricken to BELINDA and makes her own entrance.) ————— *(Enter MRS. CLACKETT, holding another plate of sardines.)*

(BROOKE enters from the dressing rooms, wearing a leopard-skin overcoat and stuffing possessions into an overnight bag. She picks up her single flower from the floor, hurls it down again in front

MRS. CLACKETT. Oh, yes, dear, it's all nice and paranormal.

ROGER. I mean, has anything ever dematerialized before? Has

of LLOYD, and storms out to the dressing rooms.)

(LLOYD subsides despairingly into a chair.

FREDERICK indicates that he will go after BROOKE. BELINDA insists that she will do it. She runs towards the dressing rooms with the axe, sees LLOYD taking a despairing swig of whisky, and runs back to take the bottle away from him.)

(FREDERICK smoothes his hair and buttons his jacket, and exits with determination towards the dressing rooms.)

(BELINDA looks to see how much LLOYD has drunk, puts it out of his reach, runs towards the dressing rooms, realizes SELSDON has picked up the whisky, and runs back.)

(Enter TIM from the dressing rooms with a third, very small bunch of flowers. He gives them to LLOYD, but BELINDA shows LLOYD SELSDON concealing the whisky about his person, and LLOYD goes to deal with him, then comes back to give BELINDA the flowers so as to leave his hands free. SELSDON quickly conceals

anything ever … *(He sees the television set on the sofa.)* … flown about?

(MRS. CLACKETT puts the sardines down on the telephone table, moves the television set back, and closes the front door.)

MRS. CLACKETT. Flown about? No, the things move themselves on their own two feet, just like they do in any house.

ROGER. I'd better warn the prospective tenant. She is inspecting the study.

(He opens the study door and then closes it again.)

ROGER, There's a man in there!

MRS. CLACKETT. No, no, there's no one in the house, love.

ROGER. *(Opening the study door.)* Look! Look!

the whisky in the fire bucket.)

(LLOYD searches SELSDON. SELSDON demonstrates that his hands are empty.)

(BELINDA hands the axe to TIM and gives LLOYD a grateful kiss for the flowers.)

(Enter FREDERICK triumphantly from the dressing rooms, bringing a reluctant BROOKE back, still in her overcoat and carrying the holdall.

She reluctantly starts to take the overcoat off, then peers at the spectacle of BELINDA, with flowers, kissing LLOYD.)

(TIM, seeing this as he takes his raincoat off, puts the raincoat back on again, hands the axe to LLOYD, and wearily holds out his hand for money.)

(LLOYD wearily hands the axe to FREDERICK and gives TIM his last small change.)

(Exit TIM to the dressing rooms. BELINDA suddenly realizes that her flowers are attracting jealous attention, and puts them on POPPY's table with the other flowers.)

ROGER. He's... *searching for* something.

MRS. CLACKETT. *(Glancing briefly.)* I can't see no one.

ROGER. You can't see him? But this is extraordinary! And where is my prospective tenant? I left her in there! She's gone! My prospective tenant has disappeared!

(He closes the study door, and looks round the living room. He sees the sardines on the telephone table.)

ROGER. Oh my God.

MRS. CLACKETT. Now what?

ROGER. There!

MRS. CLACKETT. Where?

ROGER. The sardines!

MRS. CLACKETT. Oh, the sardines.

ROGER. You can see the sardines.

MRS. CLACKETT. I can see

(BROOKE is amazed and even more upset to see that the flowers are in fact for POPPY. She puts her overcoat back on and turns to walk out again.)

(LLOYD stops her, and looks desperately round for some other token of his affection to give her instead of the flowers.)

(FREDERICK, tidily putting the axe back on the fire point, finds the whisky in the fire bucket and holds it aloft — another bottle! SELSDON takes the bottle from FREDERICK, but LLOYD takes it from SELSDON in time for...

... SELSDON to make his entrance.)

(LLOYD gives the whisky to BROOKE, kisses her, and tries to persuade her out of her overcoat while she peers at the bottle.)

(FREDERICK takes the whisky

the sardines.

(ROGER touches them cautiously, then picks up the plate.)

MRS. CLACKETT. I can see the way they're going, too.

ROGER. I'm not letting these sardines out of my hand. But where is my prospective tenant?

(He goes upstairs, holding the sardines.)

MRS. CLACKETT. I'm going to be opening sardines all night, in and out of here like a cuckoo on a clock.

(Exit MRS. CLACKETT into the service quarters.)

ROGER. Vicki! Vicki!

(Exit ROGER into the mezzanine bathroom.)

(Enter BURGLAR from the study, carrying an armful of silver cups, etc.)

BURGLAR No, I miss the violence. I miss having other human beings around to terrify.

(He dumps the silverware on the

out of BROOKE's hands.)

*(LLOYD takes it back and hands
it to BROOKE. FREDERICK
takes it away again to show it to
DOTTY, turning her round to
show her that it came from the
fire bucket, just as...*

... GARRY makes his exit ———
*and sees DOTTY now apparently
being hugged by FREDERICK.)*

*(GARRY leans down from the
platform and tips the plate of
sardines he is carrying over
DOTTY's head. Everyone, even
BROOKE, half in and half out
of her coat, watches, hands
helplessly upraised.)*

(GARRY makes his entrance.) ———

*(DOTTY puts the whisky down
on the steps to deal with the
sardines on her head.)*

(GARRY makes his exit ———
*then picks up the whisky and takes
a swig, very pleased with himself.)*

*(While GARRY stands on the
platform with his head back,
DOTTY climbs on a chair and
ties his shoelaces together.*

sofa, and exits into the study.)

*(Enter ROGER from mezzanine
bathroom.)*

ROGER. Where's she gone?
Vicki?

*(Exit ROGER into the linen
cupboard.)*

*(Enter BURGLAR from the study,
carrying PHILIP's box and bag.
He empties the contents of the box
out behind the sofa, and loads the
silverware into the box.)*

BURGLAR. It's nice to hear
a bit of shouting and screaming
around you. All this silence gets
you down.

*(Enter ROGER from the linen
cupboard, still holding the
sardines.)*

ROGER. *(Calls.)* Vicki! Vicki!

(Exit ROGER into the bedroom.)

BURGLAR I'm going to end
up talking to myself...

*(Exit the BURGLAR into study,
unaware of ROGER.)*

Everyone, even BROOKE, watches, horrified.)

(Enter PHILIP from the downstairs bathroom. His right hand is still stuck to the tax demand, his left to the plate of sardines.)

PHILIP. Darling, this stuff that eats through anything. It eats through *trousers!*

(He examines holes burnt in the front of them.)

(LLOYD tries to warn GARRY. GARRY brushes him aside because he has an entrance coming up.)

PHILIP, Darling, if it eats through trousers, you don't think it goes on and eats through... Listen, darling, I think I'd better get these trousers off! *(He begins to do so, as best he can.)* Darling, I think I can feel it! I think it's eating through... absolutely everything!

(GARRY puts the whisky down and...

... makes his entrance ——— (Enter ROGER from the bedroom, falling headlong over his feet.) *still holding the sardines.)*

ROGER. There's something evil in this house.

(DOTTY demonstrates to BELINDA and LLOYD what she did, half delighted and half shocked at herself.)

(PHILIP pulls up his trousers.)

PHILIP. *(Aside.)* The Inland Revenue!

ROGER. *(Sees PHILIP, frightened.)* He's back!

(Everyone tries to see what's

*happening on stage, also half
delighted and half shocked.)*

*(SELSDON finds the bottle on the
platform — yet another bottle!)*

*(LLOYD takes the whisky away
from SELSDON mechanically.)*

*(LLOYD, DOTTY, and BELINDA
all take swigs from it in turns,
absentmindedly, as they follow
events on stage.)*

*(DOTTY holds up her hand to get
attention to the events on stage.
She demonstrates that GARRY is
going to have to run downstairs.)*

(They all wait for the crash.)

PHILIP. I must go.

ROGER. Stay!

PHILIP. I won't, thank you.

ROGER. Speak!

PHILIP. Only in the presence
of my lawyer.

ROGER. Only in the presence
of your... ? Hold on. You're not
from the other world!

PHILIP. Yes, yes — Marbella!

ROGER. You're some kind of
intruder!

PHILIP. Well, nice to meet you.

*(He waves goodbye with his right
hand, then sees the tax demand on
it, and hurriedly puts it away
behind his back.)*

PHILIP. I mean, have a sardine.

*(He offers the sardines on his left
hand. His trousers, unsupported,
fall down.)*

ROGER. No, you're not!
You're some kind of sex maniac!
You've done something to Vicki!
I'm going to come straight

downstairs...

(The sound of GARRY falling downstairs. ————— *(ROGER falls downstairs.)*
Even SELSDON can hear it.)

(No sound from the stage. Everyone listens, and as they listen the laughter dies away.)

(FREDERICK, on stage, improvises a line.) ————— FREDERICK. Are you all right?

(No reply.)

(BELINDA turns to DOTTY in horror — she's killed him! BELINDA opens the study door to go to GARRY. LLOYD restrains her.

At the sound of GARRY's voice ——— ROGER. *(Faintly.)* This is
... they all relax. plainly a matter for the police. *(Into the phone.)* Police!

(LLOYD takes another swig of whisky.)

PHILIP. I think I'll be running along.

(FREDERICK makes his exit ——— *(He runs, his trousers still round*
trousers round his ankles, hand- *his ankles, out through the front*
kerchief pressed to his nose. He *door.)*
looks into his handkerchief, and
comes over faint. BELINDA and ROGER. Come back.... ! *(Into*
DOTTY catch him.) *the phone)* Hello... police?
Someone has broken into my
(LLOYD remembers that BROOKE house! Or rather someone has
has an entrance coming up. He broken into someone's house...
attempts to peel the overcoat off No, but he's a sex maniac! I left a

her. BROOKE, recoiling from this, reverses into BELINDA and DOTTY, staggering under the weight of FREDERICK, and loses her lenses.)

(BELINDA and DOTTY drop FREDERICK and turn to deal with this next problem.)

(GARRY repeats the cue.) ——————

(GARRY appears, still hobbled, in the study doorway, and furiously repeats the cue yet again.) ——

(BELINDA, DOTTY, and LLOYD guide BROOKE, blinded and confused, and still wearing her overcoat, to the window for her entrance, cracking her head against the set on the way.)

(They watch as BROOKE falls headlong over the sofa onstage.) —

young woman here, and what's happened to her no one knows!

ROGER. And what's happened to her no one *knows*!

ROGER. No one *knows*!

(Enter VICKI through the window.)

VICKI. There's a man lurking in the undergrowth!

ROGER. *(Into the phone.)* Sorry... the young woman has reappeared. *(Hand over phone.)* Are you all right?

VICKI. No, he almost saw me!

(SELSDON suggests to DOTTY that the lenses may be in her clothes.)

ROGER. *(Into the phone.)* He almost saw her... Yes, but he's a burglar as well! He's taken our things!

VICKI. *(Finds PHILIP's bag and box.)* The things are here.

ROGER. *(Into the phone.)* So what am I saying? I'm saying, let's say no more about it. *(He puts the phone down.)* Well, put something on!

(SELSDON searches DOTTY's clothes. She can't understand what he's after.)

VICKI. I haven't got anything!

ROGER. There must be something in the bathroom!

(He picks up the box and bag and leads the way.)

ROGER. Bring the sardines!

(She picks up the sardines.)

(GARRY comes hobbling and raging off, ————— *(Exeunt ROGER and VICKI into the downstairs bathroom.)*
his shoes still tied together. He gazes in amazement at the sight of DOTTY and SELSDON.)

(GARRY repeats the cue.) ————— ROGER. Bring the sardines!

(LLOYD realizes, and rushes SELSDON on, as FREDERICK loads him with props.) ————— *(Enter the BURGLAR from the study, and dumps more booty.)*

(GARRY moves to commit violence upon everyone in sight, but the state of his shoes prevents him from getting more than a step or two before he has to return...

... to make his entrance.) ———

(FREDERICK takes over the search in DOTTY's clothes.)

BURGLAR. Right, that's downstairs tidied up a bit. *(He starts upstairs.)* Just give the upstairs a quick going-over for them.

(Exit the BURGLAR into the mezzanine bathroom.)

(Enter VICKI holding the sardines and a white bathmat, and ROGER, carrying the box and bag, from the downstairs bathroom.)

VICKI. A *bathmat*?

ROGER. Better than nothing!

VICKI. I can't go around in front of our taxpayers wearing a *bathmat*!

(He leads the way upstairs.)

ROGER. *I'll* look in the bedroom. You look in the other bathroom.

(GARRY makes his exit ——— and is amazed to see DOTTY now apparently embracing FREDERICK.)

(Exit ROGER into the bedroom and VICKI into the mezzanine bathroom.)

(GARRY starts downstairs to attack FREDERICK. But he is still hobbled, and in any case...

FREDERICK has to make his entrance.) —————— *(Enter PHILIP through the front door.)*

PHILIP. Darling! Help! Where are you?

(BROOKE blindly makes her entrance.) —————— *(Enter VICKI from the mezzanine bathroom.)*

(LLOYD takes over the search of DOTTY's clothing. GARRY gazes in astonishment.)

VICKI. Roger! Roger!

(Exit PHILIP hurriedly, unseen by VICKI, into the downstairs bathroom.)

(TIM enters from the dressing rooms, and hands LLOYD a cactus.)

VICKI. There's someone in the bathroom now!

(VICKI runs towards the bedrooms, then stops.)

(FLAVIA watches this anxiously.) ——— FLAVIA. *(Off.)* Oh, darling, I'm finding such lovely things!

(LLOYD hands the cactus to DOTTY without looking at it while he searches.)

(VICKI turns and runs downstairs instead, as FLAVIA enters along the upstairs corridor, absorbed in the china tea service she is carrying.)

(GARRY hobbles downstairs, takes the cactus from the distracted DOTTY, and rams it into LLOYD's bottom. Then he hobbles back upstairs, still holding the cactus.)

(VICKI exits hurriedly into the downstairs bathroom.)

FLAVIA. Do you remember this china tea service —

(LLOYD tries to pursue him...

... but stops with a cry of pain. —— (VICKI screams, off.)

FLAVIA. — that you gave me on the very first anniversary of our... ?

(GARRY puts the cactus down on the platform. He takes the ends of the black and white bed sheets that are hanging up outside the bedroom door, waiting for FREDERICK and BROOKE, and ties them together.)

(Enter VICKI from the downstairs bathroom. She stops at the sight of FLAVIA.)

FLAVIA. Who are you?

VICKI. Oh *no* — it's his wife and dependents! *(She puts her hands over her face.)*

(Enter PHILIP from the downstairs bathroom, still with his hands encumbered, holding the bathmat now as well, and keeping his trousers up with his elbows.)

PHILIP. Excuse me, I think you've dropped your dress.

(FLAVIA gasps. PHILIP looks up at the gallery and sees her.)

PHILIP. *(To FLAVIA.)* Where have you been? I've been going mad! Look at the state I'm in!

(He holds up his hands to show FLAVIA the state he is in, and his trousers fall down. The tea service slips from FLAVIA's horrified hands, and rains down

on the floor of the living room below. PHILIP hurries towards the stairs, trousers round his ankles, his hands extended in supplication.)

PHILIP. Darling, honestly!

(BROOKE makes her exit.) ——— *(VICKI flees before him, comes face to face with FLAVIA, and takes refuge in the linen cupboard.)*

(BROOKE begins to take off her overcoat.)

PHILIP. She just burst into the room and her dress fell off!

(GARRY picks up the cactus, but then has to hand it BROOKE. She peers at it, baffled, while...

(Exit FLAVIA., with a cry of pain, along the upstairs corridor.)

... GARRY makes his entrance. —— *(Enter ROGER from the bedroom, directly in PHILIP's path.)*

(BROOKE comes down from the platform holding the cactus, then stops in amazement, overcoat half on and half off, at the sight of LLOYD lowering his trousers and DOTTY pulling needles out of his bottom.)

(PHILIP holds up the bathmat in front of his face. He is invisible to ROGER, though, because the latter is holding up a white bed sheet.)

ROGER. Here, put this sheet on for the moment while I see if there's something in the attic.

(GARRY makes his exit ——— *(ROGER leaves PHILIP with the and also watches the scene sheet and exits along upstairs below in amazement. So does corridor.)* BELINDA.)*

(PHILIP turns to go back downstairs.)

(Enter BURGLAR from the mezzanine bathroom, holding two gold taps.)

BURGLAR. One pair gold taps...

(GARRY hobbles downstairs and takes the cactus from BROOKE for use against LLOYD again.)

(He stops at the sight of PHILIP.)

BURGLAR. Oh, my Gawd!

PHILIP. Who are you?

BURGLAR. Me? Fixing the taps.

(TIM warns LLOYD about GARRY.)

PHILIP. Tax? Income tax?

(LLOYD quickly pulls up his trousers.)

BURGLAR That's right, governor. In come new taps ... out go old taps.

(Exit BURGLAR into the mezzanine bathroom.)

(TIM takes the cactus from GARRY. GARRY snatches it back, then has to hand it back to TIM anyway so that he can grab VICKI's dress from its hook and...

PHILIP. Tax-inspectors everywhere!

ROGER. *(Off.)* Here you are!

PHILIP. The other one!

(Exit PHILIP into the bedroom, holding the bathmat in front of his face.)

... make his entrance. —————— *(Enter ROGER along the upstairs*

(LLOYD lowers his trousers again for DOTTY to resume operations.)

(GARRY makes his exit... ——

... and LLOYD hurriedly decides that he needs no further attention.)

(FREDERICK makes his exit —— *and picks up the bed sheets which are waiting for him and BROOKE to put on. He flaps them at BROOKE to remind her about her change. LLOYD points out the flapping sheets to her, but she puts the overcoat back on to storm out again. LLOYD retains her desperately while he takes the cactus from TIM and gives it to her as a token of his enduring affection. She peers at it, and he takes in the nature of the present for the first time himself. He turns in pained query to TIM, who gestures that it was all the shop*

corridor, holding a holding VICKI's dress.)

ROGER. I've found your dress! It came flying out of the attic at me!

——*(Exit ROGER into mezzanine bathroom.)*

(Enter PHILIP from the bedroom, trying to pull the bathmat off his head.)

PHILIP. Darling! I've got her dress stuck to my head now!

(Enter ROGER from the mezzanine bathroom.)

——*(Exit PHILIP into the bedroom.)*

ROGER. Another intruder!

(Enter the BURGLAR from the mezzanine bathroom.)

BURGLAR. Just doing the taps, governor.

ROGER. Attacks? Not attacks on women?

BURGLAR Try anything, governor, but I'll do the taps on the bath first.

had left — all the rest of their stock is now on POPPY's desk.)

(Exit BURGLAR into the mezzanine bathroom.)

ROGER. Sex maniacs everywhere! Where is Vickie? Vickie... ?

(LLOYD takes the cactus back and kisses it, with painful results, to present to BROOKE again. FREDERICK flaps the sheets in desperation.)

(Exit ROGER into the downstairs bathroom.)

(Enter BURGLAR from the mezzanine bathroom, heading for the front door.)

(BROOKE hesitates. Finally she takes off her overcoat runs up the steps with the cactus.)

BURGLAR. People everywhere! I'm off. A tax on women? I don't know, they'll put a tax on anything these days.

(Enter ROGER from the downstairs bathroom. The BURGLAR stops.)

ROGER. If I can't find her, you're going to be in trouble, you see.

BURGLAR. WC? I'll fix it.

(SELSDON makes his exit.) ——— *(Exit BURGLAR into the mezzanine bathroom again.)*

(BROOKE pushes the cactus into SELSDON's hands as she passes.)

ROGER. Vickie... ?

(There is a swirl of sheets as FREDERICK attempts to dress BROOKE in time for her entrance.)

(Exit ROGER through the front door.)

*(FREDERICK and BROOKE
make their separate entrances* —— *(PHILIP attempts to enter from
and discover that they are unable   the bedroom.)
to because their sheets are at-
tached to each other.)*

*(BELINDA, upstairs for her en-
trance, goes to disentangle them.
So does SELSDON, but he and the
cactus together makes things
worse.)*

*(FREDERICK and BROOKE
 are half on and half off.)* ——————— *(VICKI attempts to enter from the
                                         linen cupboard.)*

*(GARRY watches with pleasure,
until LLOYD furiously drives
him...*

... on stage to hold the fort. ——————— *(Enter ROGER through the front
                                           door.)*

(GARRY improvises.) ——————————— ROGER. No sheikh yet! I
                                         thought he was coming at four? I
(TIM takes off his raincoat and   mean, it's nearly, you know, four
starts to put on the spare sheet   now... Well, it's after three...
to go on as FREDERICK's   Because I've been standing here
double. LLOYD rips it off him   for a good, you know, it seems
again, and gestures that it's   like forever... What's the time
needed as an emergency substi-   now. It must be getting on for
tute for FREDERICK's sheet.   *five...*
*They pass to the sheet to FRE-
DERICK, but he is too entangled
to do anything with it.)*

*(BELINDA gestures desperately
to LLOYD for the real SHEIKH's*

robes. LLOYD passes them up to
BELINDA, who hands them to
FREDERICK...

... who is dragged on through
the linen cupboard door ———— — ROGER. Oh, you're here al-
by BROOKE, still holding the already, hiding in the, anyway...
second sheet and the real And this is your charming wife?
SHEIKH's robes.) So you want to see over the house
now, do you, Sheikh? Right. Well.
(FLAVIA takes the cactus away Since you're upstairs already —
from SELSDON, then hurriedly
hands it down to LLOYD so *(ROGER goes upstairs.)*
that...

... she can make her entrance. ——(Enter FLAVIA along the upstairs
corridor, carrying a vase.)

FLAVIA. Him and his floozie!
(LLOYD puts the cactus in a safe I'll break this over their heads!
place on the chairs downstairs.)
(ROGER, PHILIP and VICKI go
downstairs.)

(TIM puts on the bathmat as ROGER. *(To PHILIP and*
burnous, to go on as PHILIP's *VICKI.)* I'm sorry about this. I
double, but gestures to LLOYD don't know who she is. No
that he now has no sheet to wear, connection with the house, I
because it has vanished on stage assure you.
with FREDERICK.)
(Enter MRS. CLACKETT from
(They both register despair.) *the service quarters, with another*
plate of sardines. ROGER.
(LLOYD takes a despairing pull *advances to introduce her.)*
of whisky.)
MRS. CLACKETT. No other
hands, thank you, not in my

sardines, 'cause this time I'm eating them.

(ROGER ushers PHILIP and VICKI away from MRS. CLACKETT towards the mezzanine bathroom.

He opens the door to the mezzanine bathroom.)

ROGER. But in here...

FLAVIA. *Arab* sheets?

(BELINDA exits.) ——————— *(Exit FLAVIA into the bedroom.)*

ROGER. In here we have...

(LLOYD and TIM indicate the problem of the missing sheet to her.)

(Enter the BURGLAR from the mezzanine bathroom.)

BURGLAR. Ballcocks, governor. Your ballcocks have gone.

(She instantly indicates TIM's own raincoat.

ROGER. We have him.

LLOYD puts it on TIM back to front.

(Enter FLAVIA from the bedroom.)

They both gloomily inspect the result.)

MRS. CLACKETT. You give me that sheet, you devil!

(She seizes the nearest sheet, and it comes away in her hand to reveal VICKI.)

(FLAVIA comes downstairs

menacingly.)

*(FREDERICK makes his exit ——— (Exit PHILIP discreetly into the
dragging BROOKE backwards study.)
with him, since they are still at-
tached to each other.)*

(SELSDON improvises a line. ——— BURGLAR. It's my little girl!
So far as I could see before she
went.

*(BROOKE struggles back on as
best she can.) ———————* VICKI. Dad!

(FLAVIA stops.)

*(TIM makes his entrance in
back-to-front raincoat.) ———(Enter PHILIP from the study in
amazement. [He is now played by
a double — TIM.])*

(FREDERICK has picked up the   BURGLAR Our little Vicki,
real burnous, and flaps it in des- that ran away from home, I
peration as he realizes that the thought I'd never see again!
*robes are still somewhere on-
stage.*   FLAVIA. *(Threateningly.)* So
where's my other sheet?
*All LLOYD can find now as a sub-
stitute is BROOKE's leopard-skin
overcoat. He spins FREDERICK
round to put it on him back to
front, as he did with TIM and the
raincoat. He then crams the
burnous on FREDERICK's head,
but FREDERICK has continued
to turn, so it hangs over his face
instead of his neck. LLOYD
crams the SHEIKH's dark
glasses on top of the burnous...*

... and FREDERICK stumbles blindly back on stage.) ————— *(Enter through the front door a SHEIKH, played by FREDERICK.)*

(LLOYD picks up the whisky, takes a weary swig, and is just about to sit down on the cactus when he springs up again guiltily, because POPPY is standing agitatedly in front of him.

She takes the whisky away from him and puts it down, desperate to secure his full attention. She whispers urgently to him. He can't understand. She whispers again, becoming more and more agitated. He puts a hand to his ear, meaning he can't hear.)

SHEIKH. Ah! A house of heavenly peace! I rent it!

ROGER. Hold on, hold on... I know that face! *(Pulls the SHEIKH's burnous aside to reveal his face.)* He isn't a sheikh! He's that sex-maniac!

(They all fall upon him, and reveal that his trousers are around his ankles.)

BURGLAR. And what you're up to with my little girl down there in Basingstoke I won't ask. But I'll tell you one thing, Vicki.

VICKI. What's that, Dad?

BURGLAR When all around is strife and uncertainty, there's nothing like a...

(He dries.)

POPPY. *(Screams to LLOYD in despair)* I'm going to have a...

(SELSDON flings the front door open.)

SELSDON. Good old-
fashioned plate of *what*...?

POPPY. ... *baby*!

> *(Everyone on stage gasps. Their
> heads flick round, then back
> again.)*

(SELSDON goes back on stage.) —— SELSDON. A good old-
fashioned plate of gravy!

*(POPPY claps her hand over her
mouth, horrified.)*

LLOYD. *(Whispers.)* And curtain, perhaps?

POPPY. Oh...!

*(She runs back to the corner to
bring the curtain down.)* ————————CURTAIN

*(LLOYD subsides, defeated, on
to the cactus, and springs up
again in agony.)*

*(Everyone appears in the doors
and windows, eager to know
more.)*

CURTAIN

ACT III

The curtain goes up to reveal the tabs of the Municipal Theatre, Stockton-on-Tees. A half-empty whisky bottle nestles at the foot of them. The introductory music for Nothing On.

(As the music finishes the tabs begin to rise. A foot or two above stage level they stop uncertainly, hover for a moment, and fall again.
Pause.
The introductory music starts again, and is then faded out.
Enter TIM from the wings, in his dinner jacket, but with elements of the BURGLAR's gear visible beneath it, and the BURGLAR's cap on his head.)

TIM. Good evening, ladies and gentlemen. *(He removes the BURGLAR's cap.)* Welcome to the Old Fishmarket Theatre, Lowestoft, or rather the Municipal Theatre, Stockton-on-Tees, for this evening's performance of *Nothing On*. We apologize for the slight delay in starting tonight, which is due to circumstances...

BELINDA. *(Off, screaming but indistinguishable.)* Hands off Freddie! All right?

DOTTY. *(Off, screaming but indistinguishable.)* You're the one who's trying to get their hands on Freddie!

TIM. ... due to circumstances...

DOTTY. *(Off, screaming but indistinguishable.)* You don't own him, you know!

TIM. ... beyond our control... *(The sound of a slap, off, and DOTTY screams in pain, off.)* ... and we would ask you to bear with us for a moment while we deal with her. With them. With the circumstances. I should perhaps say with tonight's performance of the play our long and highly successful tour...

POPPY. *(Over Tannoy.)* Ladies and gentlemen. We apologize for the delay in starting tonight, which is due to circumstances which have...

BELINDA. *(Over Tannoy.)* Don't you dare! Don't you dare!

POPPY. *(Over Tannoy)* ... which have now been brought under control.

TIM. ... our long and highly successful tour is on its very last legs. Its very last leg. Thank you for your...

POPPY. Thank you for your...

TIM and POPPY. *(Together.)* ... co-operation and understanding.

TIM. I sincerely trust... *(He pauses for an instant to see if he will be interrupted again.)* I sincerely trust there will be no other... *(He becomes aware of the whisky bottle.)* ... no other hiccups. No other holdups. So, ladies and gentlemen, will you please sit back and enjoy the remains of the evening.

(Exit TIM. A slight pause, then his arm comes out from under the tabs and retrieves the bottle.

The introductory music for Nothing On, *and this time the tabs rise. The act is being seen from the front again, exactly as it was the first time, at the rehearsal in Weston-super-Mare.*

Enter slowly and with dignity from the service quarters, limping painfully, MRS. CLACKETT. She is holding a plate in her left hand and a handful of loose sardines in her right.)

MRS. CLACKETT. *(Bravely.)* It's no good you going on... *(She stops and looks at the phone. It hurriedly starts to ring.)* I can't pick sardines off the floor *and* answer the phone. *(She dumps the handful of sardines on the plate.)* I've only got one leg. *(She shifts the plate to her right hand and picks up the phone with the left. Into the phone, bravely.)* Hello... Yes, but there's no one here... No, Mr. Brent's not here... *(She puts the plate of sardines newspaper down next to the newspaper on the sofa as she speaks and picks up the newspaper. She shakes the outer sheet free and wipes her oily hand on it as best she can. The rest of the newspaper disintegrates and falls back on top of the sardines.)* He lives here, yes, but he don't live here now because he lives in Spain. Mr. Philip Brent, that's right... The one who writes the plays, only why he wants to get mixed up in plays God only knows, he'd be safer off in the lion's cage at the zoo... No, she's in Spain, too, they're all in Spain, there's no one here... Am *I* in Spain...? *(She realizes that she is holding the sheet of newspaper instead of the sardines. She turns round to look for them as she speaks, winding herself into the telephone cord.)* No, I'm not in Spain, dear. I look after the house for them, but I go home at one o'clock on Wednesday, only I've got a nice plate of sardines to put my feet up with... *(She sits down uncertainly on the heap of newspaper.)* ... because it's the royal what's it called on the telly — the royal you know... *(She realizes that she is sitting on the sardines, and extracts the plate as discreetly as possible as she speaks.)* ... And if it's to do with letting the house then you'll have to ring the house agents, because they're the agents for the house... Squire, Squire, Hackham and who's the other one...? *(She examines the flattened contents of the plate.)* No, they're not in Spain, they're just a bit squashed. Squire, Squire, Hackham, and hold on... *(She stands up to go, uncertainly balancing plate, sheet of newspaper, and phone.)* ... I'm going to do something wrong here. *(She starts to go, then realizes there are loose sheets of newspaper all over the floor, and bends down to picks them up. The sardines slide off the plate on to the floor.)* Always the same, isn't it. *(She starts to go again.)* One minute you've got too much on your plate... *(She realizes that she has nothing on her plate, turns round and sees the sardines.)* ... next thing you know they've gone again.

(She uncertainly drops a few sheets of the newspaper over the sardines and exits into the study, holding the empty plate and the telephone receiver. The body of the phone falls off its table and follows her to the door.)
The sound of a key in the lock. The front door opens. On the doorstep is ROGER, carrying a cardboard box.)

ROGER. ... I have a housekeeper, yes, but this is her afternoon off. *(Enter VICKI. The body of the phone begins to creep inconspicuously towards the door.)* So we've got the place entirely to ourselves. *(ROGER goes back and brings in a flight bag and closes the front door.)* I'll just check. *(He halts the telephone with a casually placed foot. VICKI gazes round.)* Hello? Anyone at home? No, there's no one here. *(He picks the phone up, and puts it back on its table.)* So what do you think?

(He takes his hand off the phone, and it springs back on to the floor.)

    VICKI. Great. And this is all yours?

(The phone starts to creep away again. ROGER casually picks it up as he talks and puts it down on the sideboard.)

    ROGER. Just a little shack in the woods, really. Converted posset mill. Sixteenth-century.
    VICKI. It must have cost a bomb.

(Another jerk on the wire catapults the phone across the room. VICKI pays no attention to it.)

    ROGER. Well, one has to have somewhere to entertain one's business associates. Someone on the phone now, by the look of it. *(He picks the phone up and puts it back on the sideboard.)* It's probably this, you know, this Arab saying he wants to come at four, so I mean I'll just have a word with him and...

(He tries to pick up the receiver and finds that it's not there. As the conversation continues he follows the receiver cord along with his hand.)

    VICKI. Right, and I've got to get those files to our Basingstoke office by four.
    ROGER. Yes, we'll only just manage to pick it in. I mean, we'll only just fit it up. I mean...
    VICKI. Right, then.
    ROGER. We won't bother to pull the champagne.

(He pulls gently at the cord.)

VICKI. All these doors!

ROGER. Oh, only a handful, really. Study... Kitchen... and a self-contained service flat... *(He tugs hard, and the cord comes away without the receiver.)* ... for the receiver.

VICKI. Terrific. And which one's the... ?

ROGER. What?

VICKI. You know...

ROGER. The usual offices? Through here, through here.

(He bundles up the phone and cable, and opens the downstairs bathroom door for her.)

VICKI. Fantastic.

(Exit VICKI into the bathroom. ROGER tosses the phone casually off after her.
Enter MRS. CLACKETT from the study, still walking with difficulty and holding the now cordless receiver.)

MRS. CLACKETT. I've lost the sardines again...

(Mutual surprise. ROGER closes the door to the bathroom.)

ROGER. I'm sorry. I thought there was no one here.

MRS. CLACKETT. I'm not here. *(She looks round for the phone, so that she can replace the receiver.)* I don't know where I am.

ROGER. I'm from the agents.

MRS. CLACKETT. Lost the phone now.

ROGER. Squire, Squire, Hackham, and Dudley.

MRS. CLACKETT. Never lost a phone before.

ROGER. I'm Tramplemain.

MRS. CLACKETT. I'll just put it up here, look, if anyone wants it.

(She puts the receiver on top of the television.)

ROGER. Oh, right, thanks. No, I just dropped in to... go into a few things... *(The bathroom door opens. ROGER closes it. MRS. CLACKETT gets down on her hands and knees and looks under the newspaper.)* Well, to check some of the measurements... *(The bathroom door opens. ROGER closes it. MRS. CLACKETT goes to scoop up the sardines, but then looks round.)* Do one or two odd jobs...

(The bathroom door opens. ROGER closes it.)

    MRS. CLACKETT. Now the plate's gone.
    ROGER. Oh, and a client. I'm showing a prospective client over the house.

(The bathroom door opens.)

    VICKI. What's wrong with this door?

(ROGER closes it.)

    ROGER. She's thinking of renting it. Her interest is definitely aroused.

(Enter VICKI from the bathroom.)

    VICKI. That's not the bedroom.
    ROGER. The bedroom? No, that's the downstairs bathroom and WC suite. And this is the...

(ROGER steps forward on to the newspapers to introduce MRS. CLACKETT. His foot slides away in front of him.)

    MRS. CLACKETT. Sardines, dear, sardines.
    VICKI. Oh. Hi.
    ROGER. She's not really here.
    MRS. CLACKETT. *(Looking under the newspaper.)* Oh, you shouldn't have stood on them.
    ROGER. *(To MRS. CLACKETT.)* Don't worry about us.
    MRS. CLACKETT. They'll all go standing on them now.

ROGER. We'll just inspect the house.

MRS. CLACKETT. I'd better give the floor a wash.

(Exit MRS. CLACKETT into the study, leaving the sardines beneath the newspaper on the floor.)

ROGER. I'm sorry about this.

VICKI. That's all tight. We don't want the television, do we?

ROGER. Television? That's right, television, she didn't explain about wanting to watch this royal, you know, because obviously there's been this thing with the... *(He indicates the sardines.)* I mean, I'm just, you know, in case anyone's looking at all this and thinking, 'My God!'

VICKI. Great. Come on, then. *(She starts upstairs.)* I've got to be in Basingstoke by four.

ROGER. Sorry, love. I thought we ought to get that straight.

VICKI. We'll take it up with us.

ROGER. Where are we?

VICKI. And don't let my files out of sight.

ROGER. Hold on. We've got out of...

VICKI. What?

ROGER. What?

VICKI. Her?

ROGER. Her? OK...'her'. Right, because she *has* been in the family for generations.

(Enter MRS. CLACKETT from the study, carrying a fire bucket and a mop.)

MRS. CLACKETT. Sardines... Sardines... It's not for me to say, of course, dear, only I will just say this: don't think twice about it — take the plunge... *(She plunges the mop into the fire bucket.)* You'll really enjoy it here...

(She discovers that the mop won't go into the fire bucket.)

VICKI. Oh. Great.

(MRS. CLACKETT removes the obstruction — a bottle of whisky.)

MRS. CLACKETT. I'll put it here, look, then if he wants it he won't know where to find it...

(MRS. CLACKETT puts the bottle of whisky with the other bottles on the sideboard.)

VICKI. Terrific.
MRS. CLACKETT. Sardines, sardines. *(She hands the mop to ROGER.)* You'll have to do the sardines, then, 'cause I've got to go back to the kitchen now and do some more sardines.

(Exit MRS. CLACKETT to service quarters.)

VICKI. You see? She thinks it's great. She's even making us sardines!
ROGER. *(Contemplates the bucket and mop uncertainly.)* Well...
VICKI. I think she's terrific.
ROGER. Terrific.
VICKI. So which way?
ROGER. I don't know — kind of parcel them up in the... *(He holds out some sheets of newspaper to her.)* And I'll... *(He demonstrates the mop.)*
VICKI. *(Starts up the stairs.)* Up here?
ROGER. Down here!
VICKI. In here?
ROGER. OK, *I'll* do the... *you* do the...

(Exit VICKI into the mezzanine bathroom. ROGER parcels up the sardines in the newspaper as best he can.)

VICKI. It's another bathroom.

(She reappears.
ROGER dumps the parcel of sardines on the telephone table while he

dabs hurriedly at the floor with the mop.)

>   ROGER. Take the box upstairs, then! Take the bag!
>   VICKI. Always trying to get me into bathrooms.
>   ROGER. Bag! Box!

(VICKI moves to stand outside the airing cupboard.)

>   VICKI. Oh, black sheets!
>   ROGER. *(Runs to the stairs with bucket and mop, and holds them out to VICKI.)* All right, take the... take the... take the...!
>   VICKI. Oh, you're in a real state!
>   ROGER. *(Despairingly.)* Oh...!

(ROGER runs back and abandons the bucket and mop to pick up the bag and box.)

>   VICKI. You can't even get the door open.

(Exit VICKI into the bedroom.
ROGER runs back to collect the bucket and mop, just as the front door opens to reveal PHILIP, carrying a cardboard box.)

>   PHILIP. No, it's Mrs. Clackett's afternoon off, remember. We've got the place... *(PHILIP freezes, as ROGER flees upstairs with the bag and the box. PHILIP follows ROGER's progress out of the corner of his eye. Enter FLAVIA carrying a flight bag like GARRY's. The bedroom door shuts in ROGER's face. He opens the door again and exits into the bedroom with the bag and box.)* ... entirely to ourselves.
>   FLAVIA. Home.
>   PHILIP. Home, sweet home.
>   FLAVIA. Dear old house!
>   PHILIP. Just waiting for us to come back!
>   FLAVIA. *(Producing the remains of the phone.)* But how odd to find the telephone in the garden!
>   PHILIP. I'll put it back.

(She hands him the phone — now in a very deteriorated condition — and he attempts to replace it on the telephone table. But it is still connected to its lead, which is too short, since it runs out through the downstairs bathroom door, and back in through the front door.)

    FLAVIA. I thought I'd better bring it in.
    PHILIP. Very sensible.

(He tugs discreetly at the lead.)

    FLAVIA. Someone's bound to want it.
    PHILIP. Oh dear. *(He tugs.)*
    FLAVIA. Why don't you put it back on the table?
    PHILIP. The wire seems to be caught.
    FLAVIA. Oh, look, it's caught round the downstairs bathroom.
    PHILIP. So it is.

(PHILIP takes the phone back out of the front room. FLAVIA with discreet violence pulls the lead out of the junction-box where it originates. PHILIP reemerges with the phone through the downstairs bathroom.)

    FLAVIA. I think I've disentangled it.
    PHILIP. I climbed through the bathroom window and... oh...
oh...

(He takes the parcel of sardines off the telephone table and puts the telephone in its place.)

    FLAVIA. It's rather funny, though, creeping in like this for our wedding anniversary!
    PHILIP. It's damned serious! If Inland Revenue find out we're in the...

(Attempting to fold up the newspaper tidily, he becomes distracted by the contents that come oozing out over his hands. His voice dies away.)

FLAVIA. ... country, even for one night...

PHILIP. Sorry. *(He puts down the parcel of sardines on the sofa.)* Yes, because if Inland Revenue find out we're in the...

(He moves towards the champagne, and slides, exactly like GARRY, on the oily patch on the floor. He stops and looks back on it in surprise.)

FLAVIA. ... country...

PHILIP. *(Distracted.)* ... country...

FLAVIA. ... even for one night.

PHILIP. ... even for one night...

(PHILIP edges cautiously away from the oily patch.)

FLAVIA. ... bang goes... *(He bangs into the bucket and mop.)* ... our claim to be resident abroad...

(PHILIP fumbles for his handkerchief, and claps it to his nose.)

PHILIP. Resident abroad. Absolutely. *(He looks into his handkerchief.)*

FLAVIA. Bang goes most of this year's income.

PHILIP. Most of this year's income... *(He puts the handkerchief away.)* So, yes, I think I'd better... *(He picks up bag and box, clutches them to himself for reassurance.)* ... go and have a little lie-down.

(He starts up the stairs.)

FLAVIA. *(Surprised, but rallying)* Lie-down, yes, well, why not? No children. No friends dropping in... *(She moves the sofa to cover the oily patch as she speaks.)* We're absolutely on our... Leave those!

PHILIP. Oh, yes.

(PHILIP puts the bag and box down, but by this time he is already upstairs.)

FLAVIA. Downstairs! Not upstairs!

PHILIP. I'm so sorry. I... *(He looks in his handkerchief again.)*
Oh dear...

(He exits hurriedly into bedroom.)

FLAVIA. *(Picks up the fire bucket and mop.)* There is something to be said for being a tax exile... *(She flees upstairs with the fire
bucket and mop, laughing.)* Sh...! What? Inland Revenue may hear us!

*(Enter MRS. CLACKETT from the service quarters carrying a fresh
      plate of sardines.)*

MRS. CLACKETT. *(To herself.)* What I did with that first lot
of sardines I shall never know.

*(She puts down the plate of sardines, and goes to sit on the sofa, on
      the parcel of sardines left there by PHILIP.)*

FLAVIA. *(Urgently, looking down from the gallery, still holding the bucket and mop.)* Mrs. *Newspaper*!

(MRS. CLACKETT jumps up.)

MRS. CLACKETT. Oh, you give me a turn! My heart jumped
right out of the sofa!

FLAVIA. So did mine! We thought you'd gone!

MRS. CLACKETT. *(Finding the parcel of sardines and exam-
ining it.)* I thought you was in Sardinia!

FLAVIA. We are! We are! You haven't seen us! We're not
here!

MRS. CLACKETT. I can guess which one of them put this
here.

FLAVIA. Yes, but the main thing is that the income tax are after us.

MRS. CLACKETT. Lovely helping of sardines to sit on.

FLAVIA. So if anybody asks for us, you don't know nothing.

Anything. So I'll just... I'll just... get a hot water bottle.

(She goes towards the mezzanine bathroom.)

MRS. CLACKETT. And off she goes without waiting to find out about his letters.
FLAVIA. *(Stops, realizes despairingly.)* His letters?

(Enter PHILIP groggily from the bedroom.)

PHILIP. Letters? What letters? You forward all the mail, don't you?
MRS. CLACKETT. Not presents from Sardinia, dear.
PHILIP. I'm so sorry.

(Exit PHILIP into the bedroom.)

MRS. CLACKETT. I'll show you where I put presents from Sardinia. *(She goes upstairs towards FLAVIA who is still outside the mezzanine bathroom, carrying the bucket and mop, not sure which way to move.)* I put presents from Sardinia in the pigeonhouse.
FLAVIA. In the *pigeonhouse*?
MRS. CLACKETT. In the little pigeonhouse down here, love.

*(She stuffs the parcel of sardines down the front of FLAVIA's dress.
FLAVIA looks down at the dress, then at the fire bucket and mop
she is carrying. MRS. CLACKETT retires hurriedly back downstairs, and exits into the study, with FLAVIA after her.
Enter ROGER from the bedroom, still dressed, but with no tie on.)*

ROGER. Yes, but I could hear voices!

*(He falls over PHILIP's bag and box.
Enter VICKI from the bedroom in her underwear.)*

VICKI. Voices? What sort of voices?
ROGER. Box voices. I mean, *people's* boxes.

VICKI. But there's no one here.

ROGER. Darling, I saw the door handle move! And these bags... I'm not sure they were, you know, when we went into the, do you know what I mean?

VICKI. I still don't see why you've got to put your tie on to look.

ROGER. *(Picking up the bag and box.)* Because if someone left these things outside the, I mean, come on, they obviously want them downstairs inside the, you know.

VICKI. Mrs. Clockett?

ROGER. It could be. Coming up here on her way to, well, carrying various, I mean, who knows?

VICKI. *(Looking over the banisters.)* Oh look, she's opened our sardines.

(She moves to go downstairs. ROGER puts down the bag and box out side the linen cupboard and grabs her.)

ROGER. Come back!
VICKI. What?
ROGER. I'll fetch them! You can't go downstairs like that.
VICKI. Why not?
ROGER. Mrs. Crackett.
VICKI. Mrs. Crackett?
ROGER. One has certain obligations.

(Enter MRS. CLACKETT from the study, fishing sardines out of the front of her dress.)

MRS. CLACKETT. *(To herself.)* Sardines here. Sardines there. It's like the Battle of Waterloo out there. *(ROGER tries to pull open the linen cupboard door to conceal VICKI, but it is obstructed by the bag and box.)* Oh, you're still poking around, are you?

ROGER. Yes, still poking, well, still pulling.

(He tugs at the door again, unaware of the obstruction, and the handle comes off as it opens.)

MRS. CLACKETT. Good job I can't see far with this leg.

(ROGER moves the bag and box, gets VICKI inside the linen cupboard, and rebalances the handle in place.)

ROGER. Just, you know, trying all the doors and I mean checking all the door handles. *(He starts downstairs, carrying PHILIP's bag and box.)* Mrs. Blackett.
MRS. CLACKETT. Clackett, dear, Clackett.
ROGER. Mrs. Clackett. Is there anyone else in the house, Mrs. Clackett?
MRS. CLACKETT. I haven't seen no one, dear.
ROGER. I thought I heard a box. I mean, I found these voices.
MRS. CLACKETT. Voices? There's no voices here, love.
ROGER. I must have imagined it.
PHILIP. *(Off.)* Oh good Lord above!

(The colossal sound of PHILIP falling downstairs, off, taking half the platform with him, followed by a wailing groan.)

ROGER. I beg your pardon?
MRS. CLACKETT. *(Mimicking PHILIP.)* Oh good Lord above!

(She crashes things about on the sideboard in imitation of the offstage crash, and ends the performance with a wailing groan.)

ROGER. Why, what is it?
MRS. CLACKETT. The study door's open.

(She crosses and closes the door.)

ROGER. They're going to want these inside the... *(He indicates the study.)* So I'll put them outside the... *(He indicates the front door.)* Then they can, do you know what I mean?

*(Exit ROGER through the front door, carrying the bag and box.
Enter FLAVIA from the mezzanine bathroom, carrying a first-aid box.*

She sees the linen cupboard door swinging open as she passes, and pushes it shut, so that the latch closes. The handle comes off in her hand.)

FLAVIA. Nothing but flapping doors in this handle.

(Exit FLAVIA into the bedroom, holding the first-aid box and the handle. Enter from the study PHILIP, holding a tax demand and its envelope. The part is now being played not by FREDERICK but by TIM.)

PHILIP/TIM. '... final notice... steps will be taken... distraint... proceedings in court...'
      MRS. CLACKETT. Oh my Lord, who are you?
      PHILIP/TIM. I'm PHILIP. .
      MRS. CLACKETT. You're Philip? What happened to you?
      PHILIP/TIM. Well, it's all got a bit slippery on the stairs out there.
      MRS. CLACKETT. You haven't done himself an injury?
      PHILIP/TIM. No. He's just a bit shaken. I'll be all right in a minute. *(Exit MRS. CLACKETT to the study.)* You weren't going to tell me a gentleman had come about the house, were you?
      MRS. CLACKETT. *(Off.)* What?
      PHILIP/TIM. You weren't going to tell me a gentleman had come about the house?

(Enter MRS. CLACKETT from the study.)

MRS. CLACKETT. That's right. A gentleman come about the house.
      PHILIP/TIM. Don't tell me. I'm not here.
      MRS. CLACKETT. Oh, and he's put your box out in the garden for you.
      PHILIP/TIM. Let them do anything. Just so long as you don't tell anyone we're here.
      MRS. CLACKETT. So I'll just sit down and turn on the... sardines, I've forgotten the sardines! *(She finds the second plate of sar-*

dines on the table, exactly where she put it.) Oh, no, I haven't — I've remembered the sardines! What a surprise! I must go out to the kitchen and make another plate of sardines to celebrate.

(Exit MRS. CLACKETT to the service quarters.)

PHILIP/TIM. I didn't get this! I'm not here. I'm in Spain. But if I didn't get it I didn't open it.

(Enter FLAVIA from the bedroom. She is holding the dress that VICKI arrived in, and the handle of the linen cupboard.)

FLAVIA. Darling... *(She stares at PHILIP/TIM in surprise, then recovers herself and looks at the dress.)* I never had a handle like this, did I?
PHILIP/TIM. *(Abstracted.)* Didn't you?
FLAVIA. I shouldn't buy anything as brassy as this. *(FLAVIA drops the dress and attempts to replace the handle on the linen cupboard behind her back.)* Oh, it's not something you gave me, is it?
PHILIP/TIM. I should never have touched it.
FLAVIA. No, it's lovely.
PHILIP/TIM. Stick it down. Put it back. Never saw it.

(Exit PHILIP/TIM into study.)

FLAVIA. Well, I'll put it in the attic, if anyone else wants to have a try.

*(Exit FLAVIA along the upstairs corridor, taking the handle but leaving the dress on the floor.
Enter ROGER through the front door, without the bag and box.)*

ROGER. All right, all right... Now the study door's open again! What's going on? *(He goes towards the study, and opens and closes the door. He reacts to the sound of urgent knocking overhead.)* Knocking. *(Knocking.)* Upstairs! *(He runs upstairs. Knocking.)* Oh my God, there's something in the... *(He discovers the lack of a han-*

dle.) Oh my God! *(Knocking.)* Listen! I can't, because the handle has, you know. You'll just have to... *(He demonstrates pushing. Knocking.)* Come on! Come on! *(Knocking.)* I mean, whatever it is in there. Can you hear me? Darling! *(Knocking.)* Look, don't just keep banging! There's nothing I can, I mean it won't, there's nowhere to... *(Knocking. He opens the bedroom door.)* Listen! Climb round into the... *(He indicates the bedroom)* Squeeze through the, you know, and shin down the, I mean, there must be *some* way! *(Knocking.)* Oh, for pity's sake!

(Exit ROGER into the bedroom.
Enter PHILIP from the study, holding a tax demand and an envelope.
He is now being played by FREDERICK, with a plaster on his
head.)

PHILIP. '... final notice... steps will be taken... distraint... proceedings in court...'

(Enter ROGER from the bedroom, pulling VICKI after him. PHILIP
gazes at them, baffled.)

ROGER. Oh, it's you.
VICKI. Of course it's me! You put me in here! In the dark with all black sheets and things.
ROGER. I put you in *there,* but you managed to squeeze through the, you know.
VICKI. Why did *I* lock the door? Why did *you* lock the door!
ROGER. I couldn't, I mean, look, look, it's come off!
VICKI. *Someone* locked the door!
PHILIP. Sorry.

(Exit PHILIP apologetically into study.)

ROGER. Anyway, we can't stand here like this.
VICKI. Like what?
ROGER. I mean, you know, with people going in and out.
VICKI. OK, I'll take it off.

ROGER. In here, in here!

(He ushers her into the bedroom.
Enter PHILIP cautiously from the study, holding the tax demand and
the envelope.)

PHILIP. '... final notice... steps will be taken... distraint... proceedings in court...'

(Enter ROGER from the bedroom, holding the first-aid box. He looks
up and down the landing.
Enter VICKI from the bedroom.
PHILIP stares at them.)

VICKI. Now what?
ROGER. A hot water box! *I* didn't put it there!
VICKI. *I* didn't put it there.
PHILIP. Sorry.

(Exit PHILIP into the study.)

ROGER. Someone in the bathroom, filling first aid bottles.

(Exit ROGER into the mezzanine bathroom.)

VICKI. *(Anxious.)* You don't think there's something creepy
going on?

(Exit VICKI into the mezzanine bathroom
Enter FLAVIA along the upstairs corridor.)

FLAVIA. Darling... Darling? *(Enter PHILIP cautiously from*
the study. He raises the income tax demand to speak.) Darling, are
you coming to bed or aren't you?

(Exit FLAVIA into the bedroom.
PHILIP raises his income tax demand to speak.

Enter ROGER and VICKI from the mezzanine bathroom.)

    ROGER. What did you say?
    VICKI. I didn't say anything.

(Exit PHILIP into the study.)

    ROGER. I mean, first there's the door handle. Now there's the first water box.
    VICKI. I can feel goose-pimples all over.
    ROGER. Yes, quick, get something round you.
    VICKI. Get the covers over our heads.

(ROGER is about to open the bedroom door.)

    ROGER. Just a moment. What did I do with those sardines? *(He goes downstairs. VICKI makes to follow.)* You — wait here.
    VICKI. *(Uneasily.)* You hear all sorts of funny things about these old houses.
    ROGER. Yes, but this one has been extensively modernized throughout. I can't see how anything creepy would survive oil-fired central heating and ...
    VICKI. What? What is it? *(ROGER looks round.)* What's happening?
    ROGER. The sardines. They've gone. *(He double-takes on them.)* No, they haven't. They're here. Oh. Well. My God... I mean... my God! *(He turns and starts back upstairs. FLAVIA crawls through the front door. She picks up the sardines and takes them back to the front door.)* You put a plate of sardines down for two minutes, and the last thing you expect to find, I mean, these days, the one thing you don't expect to find when you come back is a plate of, I mean that's *really* weird!
    VICKI. Perhaps there is something funny going on. I'm going to get into bed and put my head under the ...

(She freezes at the sight of the empty table outside the bedroom door.)

ROGER. Because, I mean, there they are! Exactly where I ...

(He realizes that the sardines are not there.)

VICKI. Bag ...

(ROGER goes back downstairs to investigate. VICKI runs after him. FLAVIA, unseen by GARRY, hesitates. She glances up towards the landing, reminded by the mention of the bag that she has failed to set it. She looks back at the table, realizing that ROGER now expects the sardines to be on the table.)

ROGER. No, they're not. I suppose Mrs. Sprockett must have, I mean, what *is* going on?

(He looks at VICKI. FLAVIA hurriedly replaces the sardines.)

VICKI. Bag!

(FLAVIA exits hurriedly through the front door.)

ROGER. Bag?
VICKI. Bag! Bag!

(She drags ROGER back upstairs.)

ROGER. What do you mean, bag, bag?

(ROGER looks over the banisters and sees the sardines.)

ROGER. Sardines!
VICKI. Bag! Bag! Bag!
ROGER. Sardines! Sardines!
VICKI. Bag! Bag! Bag!
ROGER. Sardines! Sardines!
VICKI. Bag! Bag! Bag!

(While ROGER is gazing at the sardines, and VICKI is looking at ROGER, the bedroom door opens, and FLAVIA puts the flight bag on the table outside.)

    ROGER. *(Tearing himself away from the sight of the sardines.)* Bag? What bag?

    VICKI. *(Gazing at the bag.)* No bag!
    ROGER. No bag?
    VICKI. Your bag! Suddenly! Here! Now — gone!
    ROGER. It's in the bedroom. *(He sees the bag.)* It was in the bedroom. I put it in the bedroom. I'll put it back in the bedroom.

(As ROGER goes to open the bedroom door it opens in front of him, and FLAVIA begins to come out carrying the box.)

    VICKI. Don't go in there!

(ROGER finds himself holding the box, with the door closing his face.)

    ROGER. The box!
    VICKI. The box?
    ROGER. They've *both* not gone!
    VICKI. Oh! My files!
    ROGER. What on earth is happening? Where's Mrs. Spratchett? *(He starts downstairs with the bag and box. VICKI follows him.)* You wait in the bedroom.
    VICKI. No! No! No!

(She runs downstairs.)

    ROGER. At least put your dress on!
    VICKI. I'm not going in there!
    ROGER. I'll fetch it for you, I'll fetch it for you!

(He puts the bag and box down at the head of the stairs, returns to the bedroom, and sees the dress on the floor.

Exit ROGER into the bedroom.)

    VICKI. Yes, quick — let's get out of here!

(Enter ROGER from the bedroom.)

    ROGER. Your dress has gone.

(As he speaks he slides the dress over the edge of the gallery with his foot to get rid of it. It falls on top of VICKI beneath, and makes her jerk her head. She feels blindly around her; her lenses have gone again.)

    VICKI. I'm never going to see Basingstoke again!
    ROGER. Don't panic! Don't panic! There's some perfectly rational explanation for all this.

(He starts downstairs, looking over the banisters, appalled at the sight of VICKI below, and falls headlong over the bag and box at the top of the stairs.
VICKI searches blindly behind the sofa for her missing lenses.
Enter PHILIP from the study. He is holding the tax demand and the envelope.)

    PHILIP. '... final notice... steps will be taken... distraint...'

(His voice dies away at the sight of ROGER lying at the bottom of the stairs.
Enter FLAVIA along the upstairs corridor, carrying further pieces of bric-a-brac.)

    FLAVIA. Darling, if we're not going to bed I'm going to clear out the attic...
    PHILIP. *(To ROGER.)* Oh dear. *(He claps a handkerchief to his nose.)*
    FLAVIA. Oh great heavens!

(She rushes downstairs.

Enter MRS. CLACKETT from the service quarters, holding another plate of sardines.)

MRS. CLACKETT. No other hands, thank you, not in my sardines... *(She sees ROGER.)* ... 'cause this time she has, she's gone and killed him!

FLAVIA. He's stunned, that's all. Keep going.

ROGER. *(Lifting his head.)* Don't panic! Don't panic!

FLAVIA. He's all right! Just keep going!

ROGER. There's some perfectly rational explanation for all this.

MRS. CLACKETT. Where are we?

ROGER. I'll fetch Mrs. Splotchett and she'll tell us what's happening...

MRS. CLACKETT. You've fetched her. I'm here.

ROGER. I've fetched Mrs. Splotchett and she'll tell us what's happening.

MRS. CLACKETT. She won't, you know.

FLAVIA. *I'll* tell you what's happening.

ROGER. There's a man in there! Yes?

FLAVIA. He's not in there, my precious — he's in here, look, and so am I.

MRS. CLACKETT. No, no, there's no one in the house, love. Yes?

FLAVIA. No, look, I know this is a great surprise for everyone. I mean, it's quite a shock for us, finding a man lying at the bottom of the stairs! *(To PHILIP.)* Isn't it, darling?

PHILIP. Oh dear. *(He looks into his handkerchief.)* Oh dear oh dear. *(He sits down hurriedly.)*

FLAVIA. But now we've all met we'll just have to... Well, we'll just have to introduce ourselves! Won't we, darling?

PHILIP. Introduce ourselves. *(He struggles to his feet, but has to sit down again.)* I'm so sorry.

FLAVIA. This is my husband. I'm afraid surprises go straight to his nose!

(VICKI rises blindly from behind sofa at her cue.)

VICKI. There's a man lurking in the undergrowth!

FLAVIA. Oh, how delightful — another unexpected guest. *(To VICKI.)* So why don't you... why don't you... see what you can see in the garden? *(She pushes VICKI out of the front door, and helps PHILIP to his feet. To PHILIP.)* And darling, you go off and get that bottle marked poison in the downstairs loo. That eats through anything.

PHILIP. *(From behind his handkerchief.)* Eats through anything. Right. Thank you. Thank you. Yes, I've heard of people getting stuck with a problem, but this is ridiculous.

(He opens the downstairs bathroom door to go off. A pane of glass drops out of the mullioned window, and an arm comes through and releases the catch. The window opens, and through it appears the BURGLAR, played by TIM.)

BURGLAR/TIM. No bars. No burglar alarms. They ought to be prosecuted for incitement.

(He climbs in, and looks round in surprise to find the room full of people.)

MRS. CLACKETT. Come in and join the party, love.

FLAVIA. A burglar! This is most exciting!

PHILIP. Oh dear, this is my fault. Because when I say, 'I've heard of people getting stuck with a problem, this is ridiculous', and I open this door...

(He opens the downstairs bathroom again. Another pane of glass drops out of the mullioned window, and an arm comes through. Enter through the window the BURGLAR, played by SELSDON.)

BURGLAR/SELSDON. No bars. No burglar alarms. They ought to be prosecuted for incitement.

(He climbs in, becoming uneasily aware of the others as he does so.)

BURGLAR/TIM. No, but sometimes it makes me want to sit

down and weep.

MRS. CLACKETT. I know, love, it's getting like a funeral in here.

BURGLAR/SELSDON. When I think I used to do banks!

FLAVIA. Just keep going.

BURGLAR/SELSDON and BURGLAR/TIM. *(Together.)* When I remember I used to do bullion vaults! What am I doing now? I'm breaking into paper bags ...

FLAVIA. Keep going.

BURGLAR/SELSDON. Stop?

FLAVIA. No, no!

BURGLAR/SELSDON. I thought the coast was clear, you see. I saw him going out to the bathroom.

FLAVIA. *(Closing the downstairs bathroom door.)* Yes, never mind, it's all right. We'll think of something.

BURGLAR/SELSDON. Oh, no, I was listening most carefully. What's it he says?

PHILIP. 'I've heard of people getting stuck with a problem, but this is ridiculous.'

BURGLAR/SELSDON. And he opened the door ...

(BURGLAR/SELSDON opens the downstairs bathroom door to demonstrate.

A third pane of glass drops out of the mullioned window, and an arm comes through. Enter through the window the BURGLAR, played by LLOYD.)

BURGLAR/LLOYD. No bars. No burglar alarms. They ought to be prosecuted for incitement.

(He climbs in, very uncertain what's happening to him. He doesn't know whether to react to the presence of the others or not.)

MRS. CLACKETT. They always come in threes, don't they.

ALL 3 BURGLARS. When I think I used to do banks! When I remember I used to do bullion vaults...

FLAVIA. Hold on! We know this man! He's not a burglar! *(She snatches LLOYD's burglar hat off.)* He's our social worker!

    ROGER. He's *what?*

    FLAVIA. He's that nice man who comes in and tells us *what to do!*

    LLOYD. *(Appalled, faintly.)* What to do?

    OTHERS. *(Firmly.)* What to do!

(LLOYD is paralyzed with stage-fright. He looks round helplessly and makes vague and ineffectual gestures.)

    SELSDON. What's he saying?

    FLAVIA. He's saying, he's saying — just get through it for doors and sardines! Yes? That's what it's all about! Doors and sardines! *(To LLOYD.)* Yes?

    LLOYD. *(Helplessly.)* Doors and sardines!

    OTHERS. Doors and sardines!

(They all try to put this into practice. PHILIP picks up the sardines and runs around trying to find some application for them. The others open various doors, fetch further plates of sardines, and run helplessly around with them. LLOYD stands helplessly watching the chaos he has created swirl around him.)

    FLAVIA. He's saying, he's saying — 'Phones and police'!

    LLOYD. Phones and police...

    PHILIP. Phone!

(PHILIP and ROGER are each handed a half of the phone.)

    ROGER. Police!

(ROGER puts the receiver to his ear. PHILIP dials.)

    FLAVIA. He's saying 'Bags and boxes.'

    OTHERS. Bags and boxes!

(Everyone runs around with the two boxes and the two bags, all help-

lessly colliding with each other and running into the furniture.)

FLAVIA. *(Decisively.)* Sheets, sheets! He's saying 'Sheets'!
LLOYD. Sheets...
OTHERS. *(Desperately.)* Sheets!

(ROGER runs out of the study door, TIM out of the front door.)

FLAVIA. He's saying 'All we want now is a nice happy ending!'

(ROGER comes back at once propelling the helpless VICKI, wrapping her in the white sheet as they go. TIM comes back simultaneously with POPPY, cramming her into the real SHEIKH's robes.)

DOTTY. *(Looking at POPPY.)* And here she is! In her wedding dress!
FLAVIA. *(Looking at VICKI.)* Yes, yes — it's their wedding day!
MRS. CLACKETT. *(Still looking at POPPY.)* It's their wedding day!
OTHERS Ah!
FLAVIA. What a happy ending!

(MRS. CLACKETT pushes POPPY to LLOYD's side. FLAVIA pushes VICKI to his other side.)

MRS. CLACKETT. Do you take this sheet to be your lawful wedded wife? If not, speak now, or forever hold your peace.

(LLOYD nods helplessly.)

SELSDON. What's he saying, what's he saying?
FLAVIA. He's saying... he's saying... 'Last line!'
SELSDON. Last line? Me?
ALL. Last line, last line!

SELSDON. When ﹖
nothing like a good old-fas

(He dries.)

ALL. *(Holding up pla*

(Tableau. Then TIM runs hur

C

(Except that it jams just above the level of their heads. As one man they seize hold of it and drag it down. A ripping sound. The curtain detaches itself from its fixings and falls on top of them all, leaving a floundering mass of bodies on stage.)

COSTUMES

S
al slacks, shirt, cardigan or sweater, socks, casual shoes.
rousers, shirt, tie, jacket, coat, socks, shoes.
Gray trousers, black roll-neck sweater, jacket similar to
Burglar's, red and white neck scarf, black beanie, white
gloves, shoes, socks.

DOTTY OTLEY (Mrs. Clackett)

Act I: Skirt, blouse, wrapover pinafore, hat/turban headscarf, tights/
stockings, slippers.

Act II: Hat/turban headscarf adapted to retain sardines.

BELINDA BLAIR (Flavia)
Light-weight, elegant suit or dress, tights, shoes.

FREDERICK FELLOWS (Philip)
White flannel trousers, navy blue blazer, white shirt, cravat, white
socks and shoes, 2 white handkerchiefs, second pair of white trousers
that drop with holes and stains.

GARRY LEJEUNE (Roger)
Dark pinstripe three-piece suit, cherry and white striped shirt, red tie,
red socks, black lace-up shoes with very long laces.

For Acts II & III: Padding for elbows, knees, hips and small of back.

BROOKE ASHTON (Vicki)
"Tarty" blue dress, black patent shoes, belt and clutch bag, tights,
sexy underwear.

SELSDON MOWBRAY (Burglar)
Dressing gown, old black roll-neck sweater, old gray flannel trousers
that drop, belt, old anorak-type jacket with large pockets, red and

white neck scarf, white gloves, black beanie, socks, old sandals.

TIM ALGOOD (Company Stage Manager)
Act I: Dirty, paint-stained sweatshirt, ditto jeans/cords, old trainers, socks, old raincoat (suitable to double for Burglar), belt with tools including a hammer.
Act II: Evening suit, evening shirt, bowtie, pink socks, black shoes.
Act III: Black roll-neck sweater, red and white neck scarf, black beanie, white gloves.

POPPY NORTON-TAYLOR (Assistant Stage Manager)
Act I: Shirt, old cardigan, jeans, soft-soled shoes, socks, man's handkerchief.
Act II: Red blouse, black and white Tartan wrapover skirt, black boots, tights.

PROPERTY LIST

Prompt script
Clipboard with notes
Pen
Front door key with label
Cactus in pot
Bouquet of flowers
Bunch of flowers with 1
    removable flower
Small posy of flowers
Small coal shovel
Tea towel
First aid box
Lint dressing and Elastoplast
Section of broken door
3 plates of sardines (stuck on)
1 trick plate, sardines stuck only
    by tails
Plate with linked sardines with
    Velcro attached
Plate with 5 loose sardines in
    gelatin
Fork
Silver bowl
Silver cups (assorted)
Tax letter
Tax final demand slip
Inland Revenue envelope
Tube of glue
Tabloid newspaper
Sunglasses
2 British Airways flight bags
2 sealed champagne bottles
    (non-practical)
Cardboard box with files
Similar cardboard box with

groceries
Similar padded cardboard box
    (Freddie, Act III)
Similar empty cardboard box
Portable radio/cassette recorder
Hot water bottle
Pair of gold taps
Folded black sheet
China figurine
Silver teapot
Large ornamental vase (rubber)
2 biscuit tins
Axe (made of latex)
Fire bucket on hook
Box of tissues
Ropes, assorted (dressing)
Anglepoise lamp
Bell push on board
Notebook and pen
Metal bin with crash tin (Poppy's
    sound effect, Act II)
Dressing TV (non-practical)
Whisky bottle
Resin whisky bottle identical to
    above
2 glasses (minimum)
Phone directories
Knocking block for Brooke
Plastic cup
Dirty cup and saucer
Telephone
Telephone with long receiver
    cable and long mains cable
    (Act III)
Broken phone casing (Act III)

PERSONAL PROPS

LLOYD
Pill bottle with 'Valium' tablets
Notebook
Watch
Pen
Wallet with notes and coins

FREDDIE
Clean handkerchief
Bloody handkerchief

TIM
Tool belt with tools, including hammer
Money
Watch

GARRY
Watch

POPPY
Bloody handkerchief

FURNITURE, ETC.

ACTS I & III
Two-seater sofa
Sideboard
Drinks shelf
Small console table (upstairs landing)
Small telephone table

ACT II
Row of assorted chairs
1 loose chair
Prompt desk
Prop table
Lighting control board
Prompt stool
Electrician's chair
Minimum 5 panes of sugar glass per show (Tissue paper for above in Act II)
2 metal framed chairs
2 wooden chairs
Saucepans, tins, etc.
Metal box with cutlery for crash (Act I)
1 white nightdress
2 white "headdresses"
Burnous
Headband
2 white "Arab" robes
1 white open robe
1 black open robe
Brooke's black "two-piece" robes

ACT I / ON STAGE

Plastic cup and dirty sauces on
    P.S. forestage
Tab unhooked
Border tucked behind header
Floor clean
Sofa in position with cushions
    neat
Phone table in position with
    phone U.S. end, receiver
    cable to P.S., directories
    underneath
Sideboard with
    1. Brass vase
    2. 'Silver' cigarette box
    3. 3 small ornaments
    4. TV, plug by socket
    5. Brass idol
    6. Cigarette box
    7. Wooden box
    8. Snuff box
    9. Ashtray
    (Drawers empty and free)

See drawing below.

Service door free and shut,
    masking behind
Study door free and shit, masking
    behind
Window 6" open, catch twisted
    correctly, masking behind
    Tissue paper in panes of window
    Sugar glass in P.S. pane
Lanterns tight against window flat
Front door free and shut, knocker
    loose
Bathroom door free and shut,
    masking behind
Book shelf with:
    Whiskey bottle one-quarter
      full with the top loose
    Dressing bottles
    4 clean bottles
    Dressing glasses
    Books straight
    P.S. and O.P. masking trucks
      in position, especially
      P.S. one

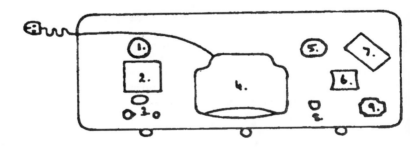

OFFSTAGE

Prompt Corner
Crash box
Taped pane of sugar glass
Phone bell working, cover off
Spare bell working
Timber for curtain call
Gaffer tape
Double-sided tape
Torch
Vacuum

U.L. Prop Table
Jug with iced water
2 – 3 glasses
Tissues
"J" cloth
Brooke's handbag
Prompt copy
Clipboard with notes and pen
Bloody handkerchief
Box for sugar glass
Door section
Cactus
Posy of flowers
Bunch with 2 trick flowers in
    tissue paper
Bouquet of flowers
Dustpan and brush
Plate with linked sardines
3 tax letters
First aid box
Small shovel
Tea towel
Act III phone done with draw crash
5 taped panes of sugar glass
Scissors

Screwdriver
Padded cardboard box
2 lint dressings with "blood"
Phone crash
Plate with 5 loose sardines
Spare tin with:
    Bottle of pills
    Handkerchiefs
    Red food color

Chairs for Artists
2 battered chairs for Act III crash

By P.S. Stair
2 metal chairs with metal object
    for crash

Back of Set
Row of 5 chairs, 4 fixed, R., end
    one loose
2 mirrors on post
Freddie's ragged trousers
Burnous
Headband

Prop Table by R. Stair
1. 3 plates of fixed sardines
2. 1 plate with attachment,
    sardines secured only by tails
3. Fork
4. Tabloid newspaper, turned to
    TV guide
5. Silver bowl with 3 cups
6. Tax letter
7. Envelope
8. Final tax demand
9. Tube of glue

See drawing on top of page 168

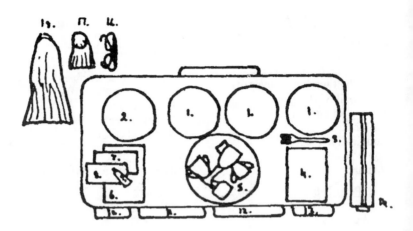

Under Table
10. Cabin bag with champagne
 bottle and padding
11. Cardboard box with groceries
 including bag with 3 apples
12. Cardboard box with files
13. Cabin bag with champagne
 bottle and padding
14. Radio/cassette recorder
15. Empty cardboard box at back

Above Table
16. Sunglasses
17. Nightdress headdress
18. Sheik's white sheet

Back of Set Upstairs, O.P. - P.S.
Bathroom door free and shut
On hooks L. of door:
　　Hotwater bottle one-third full
　　Nightdress
Gold taps on top step

Linen cupboard door free and
 shut, key in, handle secured
 with pin
Fifth shelf up:
　　Wooden knocking stick
　　Folded black sheet
　　Black sheet and headdress
　　　over rail
Bedroom door free and shut
On hooks R. of door:
　　Headdress with loops
　　White sheet robe
On hooks L. of door:
　　China figure
　　Silver teapot
On floor below hooks:
　　2 biscuit boxes
　　Rubber vase
Archway curtain straight
All maskings up and secure

Off R. Table
Box of tissues
Resin whiskey bottle with cap
    secure
Wallet with £10 note and loose
    change
Speaker
2 chairs for artists

O.P. Truck
Upstairs:
    Pint glass
    Can of beer/shandy
    Newspaper
    Cigarettes
    Matches
    Ashtray
Desk with:
    Bell unit
    Notepad
    Pen
Stool
Anglepoise lamp
Bundle of ropes
W.P.B. with biscuit tin
Axe hung with blade facing U.S.
Fire bucket with cloth and box of
    tissues
Q. lights off, master on

ACT II / ON STAGE

O.P. Truck with:
Chair
Newspaper
Cigarettes

Matches
Ashtray
Pint glass with beer/shandy
Firebucket with cloth in bottom
Fire axe on bracket, blade U.S.
Cue board with master on and
    switches off
W.P.B. with tin under fire bucket
Stool
Prompt desk with:
    Prompt copy with 2 loose pages
    Bell unit
    Anglepoise lamp, plugged up
    Notebook
    Pen
    Trail mic on clip
Under desk:
    Bundle of ropes
    Box of tissues
Under small treads:
    Freddie's ragged trousers
Row of 5 chairs
Sugar glass replaced

Prop Table by Stair
1. 3 plates of fixed sardines
2. Plate with attachment, sardines
    secured by tails
3. Tabloid newspaper, TV guide
    showing
4. Silver cup
5. Silver bowl with 2 cups
6. Tax letter
7. Tube of glue
8. Tim's coat

See drawing on top of page 170

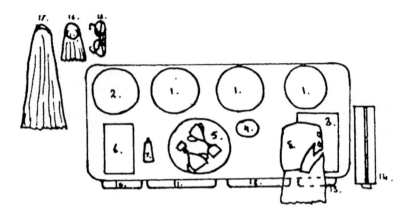

Under Table
10. Cabin bag with padding — no
    bottle
11. Empty cardboard box
12. Cardboard box with files
13. Cabin bag with padding—no
    bottle
14. Radio/cassette recorder

Above Table
15. Sungalsses
16. Nightdress headdress
17. Sheik's white sheet

Up Stairs, P.S.—O.P.
Nightdress
Hot water bottle—empty
Gold taps
Folded black sheet
Knocking stick
1 white sheet ⎱ 1 corner tied,
1 black sheet ⎰ 1 hanging free

Nightdress headdress with hoops
China figure
Silver teapot
1 biscuit box
Rubber vase

All backing down, all doors working freely and shut, window 6"
open with catch correct, LX bars
in, border in, U.S. tabs in.

Upstage Set
Sofa and table with telephone in
    position
Glass and whiskey reset as Act I
Small ornaments from sideboard
    struck
By U.S. P.S. tormentor, plate with
    linked sardines

ACT III / ON STAGE

Border tucked behind header
Carpet clean — padding under
Sofa in position, cushions neat
Phone table in position with:
> Phone with long flexes
> > (mains tacked down)
> > D.S. end
> Phone directories underneath

Behind sofa:
> Plate with 5 loose sardines on
> gelatin

Sideboard with:
1. Wooden box
2. Brass idol
3. False silver cigarette box
4. TV on Act III mark, plug on
   floor
5. Brass vase
6. Silver box

See drawing below.

Crash objects in middle drawer
Window with 4 panes of sugar
> glass, one-quarter open, catch
> correct

Lanterns straight
Front door knocker bluetacked
> down

Bookshelf with:
> No whiskey
> 4 clean glasses
> Books straight
> Dressing as Act I

All doors working freely and shut,
all maskings up, tormentors in
position, especially P.S. one

OFFSTAGE

P.S. Wing:
Various objects for Freddie to
> crash

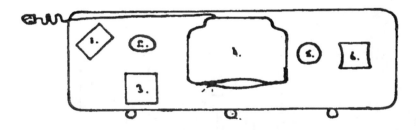

On Top of Small Treads P.S.:
 Broken phone shell
 Screwdriver
 Phone crash

Over Row of Chairs at Back:
 Black sheets — for Tim
 White sheet, headdress,
  burnous — for Poppy
 Tim's coat

Prop Table with:
1. 2 plates of sardines
2. Plate with attachment
3. Tabloid newspaper, TV guide
 showing
4. Bottle of whiskey—from
 onstage
5. Folded tea towel
6. Small shovel
7. Spare tax letter
8. Tax letter
9. Tax demand
10. Envelope
11. Tube of glue

Under table:
12. Cabin bag with padding—no
 bottle
13. Padded cardboard box
14. Cabin bag with padding—no
 bottle
15. Cardboard box with files

Above Prop Table:
16. Bloody dressings
17. Sunglasses

See drawing below

Upstairs:
Pin removed from linen cupboard
 door
Knocking block
First aid box
China figure
Silver teapot

In O.P. Wing:
2 metal chairs for crash
2 chairs for artists

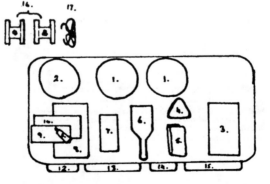

Grand Theatre

WESTON-SUPER-MARE

Proprietors: GRAND THEATRE (Weston-super-Mare) LIMITED
General Manager: E. E. A. GRADSHAW
The Grand Theatre Weston-super-Mare is a Member of the Grand Group
Evenings at 7.45
Matinee: Wednesday at 2.30
Saturday at 5.00 and 8.30

Otstar Productions Ltd present

• DOTTY OTLEY •
BELINDA BLAIR • GARRY LEJEUNE
in

NOTHING ON

by ROBIN HOUSEMONGER
with
SELSDON MOWBRAY
BROOKE ASHTON
FREDERICK FELLOWES

Directed by LLOYD DALLAS

Designed by GINA BOXHALL
Lighting by ROD WRAY
Costumes by PATSY HEMMING

•••WORLD PREMIERE•••
PRIOR TO NATIONAL TOUR!

Commencing Tuesday 15th January 1994 for One Week Only

SMOKING IS NOT PERMITTED IN THE AUDITORIUM
The use of cameras and tape recorders is forbidden.
The management reserve the right to refuse admission, also to make any alteration in the cast which
may be rendered necessary by illness or other unavoidable causes.
From the Theatre rules "All exits shall be available for use during all performances".
"The fire curtain shall be lowered during each performance".

NOTHING ON

by

ROBIN HOUSEMONGER

Cast in order of appearance:

Mrs Clackett . . . . **DOTTY OTLEY**
Roger Tramplemain . . . . **GARRY LEJEUNE**
Vicki . . . . **BROOKE ASHTON**
Philip Brent . . . . **FREDERICK FELLOWES**
Flavia Brent . . . . **BELINDA BLAIR**
Burglar . . . . **SELSDON MOWBRAY**
Sheikh . . . . **FREDERICK FELLOWES**

The action takes place in the living-room of the Brents' country home, on a Wednesday afternoon

for OTSTAR PRODUCTIONS LTD
Company & Stage Manager **TIM ALLGOOD**
Assistant Stage Manager **POPPY NORTON-TAYLOR**
Production Photographer **MARTHA NORCHEESIE**

Production credits
Sardines by Old Salt Sardines. Antique silverware and cardboard boxes by Mrs J. G. H. Norton-Taylor. Stethoscope and hospital trolley by Severn Surgical Supplies. Straitjacket by Kumfy Restraints Ltd. Coffins by G. Ashforth and Sons.

We gratefully acknowledge the generous support of **EUROPEAN BREWERIES** in sponsoring this production.

'A Glimpse of the Noumenal'

(condensed from J G Stillwater: *Eros Untrousered — Studies in the Semantics of Bedroom Farce.*)

The cultural importance of the so-called 'bedroom farce,' or 'English sex farce,' has long been recognised, but attention has tended to centre on the metaphysical significance of mistaken identity and upon the social criticism implicit in the form's ground-breaking exploration of cross-dressing and trans-gender role-playing. The focus of scholarly interest, however, is now beginning to shift to the recurrence of certain mythic themes in the genre, and to their religious and spiritual implications.

The common sardine. 13.4 million are eaten daily in Great Britain alone. The word is derived from the French, *sardine.*

In a typical bedroom farce, a man and a woman come to some secret or mysterious place (cf Beauty and the Beast, Bluebeard's Castle, etc) to perform certain acts which are supposed to remain concealed from the eyes of the world. This is plainly a variant of the traditional 'search' or 'quest', the goal of which, though presented as being 'sexual' in nature, is to be understood as a metaphor of enlightenment and transcendence. Some partial disrobing may occur, to suggest perhaps a preliminary stripping away of worldly illusions, but total nudity (perfect truth) and complete 'carnal knowledge' (i.e. spiritual understanding) are perpetually forestalled by the intervention of coincidental encounters (often with other seekers engaged in parallel 'quests'), which bear a striking resemblance to the trials undergone by postulants in various esoteric cults (cf *The Magic Flute, Star Wars*, etc).

According to evidence given to the Royal Commission on Procedures and Practice in the Sale of Real Estate, approximately 17% of estate agents admit to having on at least one occasion passed off a property they were selling as their own.

In 63% of these cases the intention was to impress a member of the opposite sex, and/or to provide accommodation for illicit sexual activity - though some witnesses had at one time or another used properties to secure a loan or other business advantage from gullible victims. One agent boasted that he had managed to have intercourse in the master bedroom, then sell his partner the property - and help himself to a case of champagne from the cellar and a pound and a half of strawberries from the garden.

A recurring and highly significant feature of the genre is a multiplicity of doors. If we regard the world on this side of the doors as the physical one in which mortal men are condemned to live, then the world or worlds concealed behind them may be thought of as representing both the higher and more spiritual plane into which the postulants hope to escape, and the underworld from which at any moment demons may leap out to tempt or punish. When the doors do open, it is often with great suddeness and unexpectedness, highly suggestive of those epiphanic moments of insight and enlightenment which give access to the 'other', and offer us a fleeting glimpse of the noumenal.

Another recurring feature is the fall or loss of trousers. This can be readily recognised as an allusion to the Fall of Man and the loss of primal innocence. The removal of the trousers traditionally reveals a pair of striped underpants, in which we recognise both the stripes of the tiger, the feral beast that lurks in all of us beneath the civilised exterior suggested by the lost trousers, and perhaps also a premonitory representation of the stripes caused by the whipping which was formerly the traditional punishment for fornication.

Posset (milk curdled with ale or vinegar) was one of the first foods to be processed by industrial methods. In the sixteenth century virtually every village had its posset-mill, though few have survived. Their functioning was based on the common observation that milk tends to curdle more readily on thundery summer days. In a posset-mill production was maintained throughout the year by allowing the milk to run into a heated curdling chamber where the flow of incoming ale or vinegar was ingeniously harnessed to operate a kind of simple theatrical thundersheet. The product was then packed in small 'yoggy pots', made from the scrota of wild yogs.

- Janet Thrice: *The Tudor Food Industry*

An early pair of
famous doubles -
Edward IV and
Leofric Leadbetter.

The confusion of identity caused by chance resemblance has always played a significant part in human affairs. Edward IV had a notorious lookalike, Leofric Leadbetter, a tallowboiler from Stony Stratford, who fooled many courtiers and visiting heads of state. Not even their wives could tell them apart. On one occasion Leadbetter gave the royal assent to three statutes and probably fathered the future King Edward V before the imposture was detected. Some historians believe that in the subsequent confusion it was in fact the king, not Leadbetter, who was hanged.

Farce, interestingly, is popularly categorised as 'funny'. It is true that the form often involves 'funny' elements in the sense of the strange or uncanny, such as supposedly supernatural phenomena, and behaviour suggestive of demonic possession. But the meaning of 'funny' here is probably also intended to include its secondary sense, 'provocative of laughter.'

Sardines are even more
plagued than their human
cousins by the problem of
doubles and lookalikes.

This is an interesting perception. It scarcely needs to be said that laughter, involving as it does the loss of self-control and the spasmodic release of breath, a vital bodily fluid, is a metaphorical representation of the sexual act. But it can also occasion the shedding of tears, which suggests that it may in addition be a sublimated form of mourning. Indeed we recognise here a symbolic foretaste of death. If sneezing has been widely feared because it is thought that during a sneeze the soul flies out of the body, and may not be recaptured (whence 'Bless you!' or 'Gesundheit!'), then how much more dangerous is laughter. Not once but over and over again the repeated muscular contractions and expulsions of breath drive the 'soul' forth from the body. The danger of laughter is recognised in such expressions as 'killingly funny,' and 'I almost died.' There is a lurking fear that even more spectacular violence may ensue, and that a farce may end with a bloodletting as gruesome as in *Oedipus* or *Medea*, if people are induced to 'split their sides' or 'laugh their heads off.'

Fear of the darker undertones of bedroom farce has sometimes in the past led to its dismissal as 'mere entertainment'. As the foregoing hopefully makes clear, though, financial support by the Arts Council or a private sponsor for the tour of a bedroom farce would be by no means out of place.

Behind the Dressing Room Doors

DOTTY OTLEY (Mrs. Clackett) makes a welcome return to the stage to create the role of Mrs. Clackett after playing Mrs. Hackett, Britain's most famous lollipop lady ('Ooh, I can't 'ardly 'old me lolly up!') in over 320 episodes of TV's *On the Zebras*. Her many stage appearances include her critically acclaimed portrayal of Fru Såckett, the comic char in Strindberg's *Scenes from the Charnelhouse*. Her first appearance ever? In a school production of *Henry IV Part I* - as the old bag-lady, Mrs. Duckett.

BELINDA BLAIR (Flavia Brent) has been on the stage since the age of four, when she made her debut in *Sinbad the Sailor* at the old Croydon Hippodrome as one of Miss Toni Tanner's Ten Tapping Tots. She subsequently danced her way round this country, Southern Africa, and the Far East in shows like *Zippedy-Dooda*! and *Here Come les Girls!* More recently she has been seen in such comedy hits as *Don't Mr. Duddle!*, *Who's Been Sleeping in My Bed?*, and *Twice Two Is Sex.* She is married to scriptwriter Terry Wough, who has contributed lead-in material to most of TV's chat shows. They have two sons and three retrievers.

> *Dignity is the straitjacket of the soul. Its loss is our first stumbling step towards sanity. - Friedrich Nietzsche*

GARRY LEJEUNE (Roger Tramplemain) while still at drama school won the coveted Laetitia Daintyman Medal for Violence. His television work includes *Police!*, *Crime Squad, Swat, Forensic*, and *The Nick*, but he is probably best-known as 'Cornetto', the ice-cream salesman who stirs the hearts of all the lollipop ladies in *On the Zebra.*

SELSDON MOWBRAY (Burglar) first 'trod the boards' at the age of 12 - playing Lucius in a touring production of *Julius Caesar*, with his father, the great Chelmsford Mowbray, in the lead. Since then he has served in various local reps, and claims to have appeared with every company to have toured Shakespeare in the past half-century, working his way up through the Mustardseeds and the various Boys and Sons of, to the Balthazars, Benvolios, and Le Beaus; then the Slenders, Lennoxes, Trinculos, Snouts, and Froths; and graduating to the Scroops, Poloniuses, and Aguecheeks. His most recent film appearance was as Outraged Pensioner in *Green Willies.*

BROOKE ASHTON (Vicki) is probably best known as the girl wearing nothing but 'good, honest, natural froth' in the Hauptbahnhofbrau lager commercial. Her television appearances range from Girl at Infants' School in *On the Zebras* to Girl in Massage Parlour in *On Pro-bation*. Cinemagoers saw her in *The Girl in Room 14,* where she played the Girl in Room 312.

> The most important technological advance in history,
> so far as the maintenance of moral standards is concerned,
> was the invention of the keyhole. - George Santayana

FREDERICK FELLOWES (Philip Brent) has appeared in many popular television series, including *Calling Casualty, Cardiac Arrest!, Out-Patients,* and *In-Patients.* On stage he was most recently seen in the controversial all-male version of *The Trojan Women.* He is happily married, and lives near Crawley, where his wife breeds pedigree dogs. 'If she ever leaves me,' he says, 'it will probably be for an Irish wolf-hound!'

ROBIN HOUSEMONGER (Author) was born in Worcester Park, Surrey, into a family 'unremarkable in every way except for an aunt with red hair who used to sing all the high twiddly bits from *The Merry Widow* over the tea-table.' He claims to have been the world's most unsuccessful gents hosiery wholesaler, and began writing 'to fill the long hours between one hosiery order and the next.' He turned this experience into his very first play, *Socks Before Marriage,* which ran in the West End for nine years. Two of his subsequent plays, *Briefs Encounter* and *Hanky Panky,* broke box office records in Perth, Western Australia. *Nothing On* is his seventeenth play.

LLOYD DALLAS (Director) 'read English at Cambridge, and stage-craft at the local benefits office.' He has directed plays in most parts of Britain, winning the South of Scotland Critics' Circle Special Award, and going on to a highly successful season for the National Theatre of Sri Lanka. In recent years he has probably be-come best known for his brilliant series of 'Shakespeare in Summer' productions in the parks of the inner London boroughs.

> Desperation tells a thousand tales - and each of those thou-
> sand begets a thousand more. - Moldovian proverb

CAUGHT IN THE NET
Ray Cooney

This sequel to *Run for Your Wife* finds the bigamist taxi driver still keeping two families in different parts of London, both blissfully unaware of the other. However, his teenage children, a girl from one family and a boy from the other, have met on the Internet and want to meet in person since they have so much in common—name, surname and taxi-driving dad! The situation spirals out of control as John juggles outrageously with the truth. "A master class in the art of farce.... A precession-built laughter machine."—*What's On*. "Brilliant.... The funniest play of the year."—*Daily Mail*. 4 m., 3 f. (#5865)

THE UNDERPANTS
Carl Sternheim / Adapted by Steve Martin

The renowned actor and author of *Picasso at the Lapin Agile* provides a wild satire based on the classic German comedy about Louise and Theo Markes, whose conservative existence is shattered when her bloomers fall down in public. She pulls them up quickly, but he fears the incident will cost him his government job. Louise's momentary display does not result in scandal but it does attract two infatuated men, each of whom wants to rent the Markes' spare room. Oblivious of their amorous objectives, Theo happily collects rent from both the foppish poet and the constantly whining hypochondriac. "Funny stuff ... a fine play ... with lightning flashes of wit."—*TheaterMania.com*. 5 m., 2 f. (#23042)

For more plays by Ray Cooney, Steve Martin and other masters of comedy, see
THE BASIC CATALOGUE OF PLAYS AND MUSICALS
online at www.samuelfrench.com

OSCAR AND FELIX
Neil Simon

America's comic mastermind has updated his classic comedy *The Odd Couple*, setting the trials and tribulations of Felix Unger and Oscar Madison in the present day. Those who love the original version as well as new audiences will laugh until they cry at this modern-day comic *tour de force*. Producers of *The Odd Couple*, the female version of *The Odd Couple* and *Oscar and Felix* are guaranteed a gleeful full house. 6 m., 2 f. (#822)

THE
INCOMPARABLE LOULOU
Ron Clark

The title character is a singer about to try for a comeback in a Staten Island nightclub. Meanwhile, LouLou's sister pushes her to publish her memoirs. The first performance is a bomb, but some of the sting is alleviated by the surprise appearance of an ex-husband who is now an up-and-coming congressman. Unfortunately, his attempt at reconciliation is only an effort to stop her from publishing certain incriminating photographs in her memoirs. "Delightful.... A confection that is irresistible."—*Miami News.* "A mine field of jokes and gags.... LouLou is pretty and delightful, vulnerable yet strong and beautiful in the way of a woman born with a natural sensuality."—*The Miami Herald.* 4 m., 3 f. (#10979)

For more plays by Neil Simon, Ron Clark
and other masters of comedy, see
THE BASIC CATALOGUE OF PLAYS AND MUSICALS
online at www.samuelfrench.com